CAROLINA'S RING

"You'll recognize the South in Lynn Seldon's crazily readable new novel, *Carolina's Ring*, but it might not be quite what you're expecting: it's more complex, more compelling, and more surprising than the 'South' as usually offered up in fiction. Full of both precision and sweep, and stretching from Chapel Hill to Charleston all the way to the furnace of Iraq, *Carolina's Ring* digs deeply into what it means to live with honor in a world lacking such."

—Mark Powell, Citadel Class of 1998, Author of *Small Treasons* and *Lioness*

"*Carolina's Ring* is an unforgettable story of love, loss, and redemption that will stay with you long after the final page is turned. As he did in his debut novel, *Virginia's Ring*, Lynn Seldon offers an authentic, behind-the-scenes look at the unbreakable bonds of friendship and loyalty forged within the military college system."

—Cassandra King, Author of *Tell Me a Story: My Life with Pat Conroy*

"Lynn Seldon's new novel is an insightful and deeply moving account of ways that duty, honor, and love merge in the lives of two brothers and the woman they have both sought. An additional (and fitting) bonus is a cameo by Pat Conroy, who, like Lynn Seldon, understood the bond of those 'who wear the ring.' Bravo!"

—Ron Rash, Author of the 2009 PEN/Faulkner Finalist and *New York Times* Bestseller *Serena* and *Above the Waterfall*, in addition to four prizewinning novels, four collections of poems, and six collections of stories

"VMI graduate, seasoned travel writer, and son of the South Lynn Seldon brings his particular knowledge to bear on this bittersweet tale of twin brothers—bound for different military institutes—and the girl they've both grown to love. As the inseparable trio come of age, their destinies unravel, overlap, and eventually intertwine as all the best Southern stories do. A protégé of the late Pat Conroy, Seldon does his mentor proud with this lyrical novel of love, loss, and loyalty."

—Margaret Shinn Evans, Editor, *Lowcountry Weekly*

"There are many components of a terrific novel: plot and place, pacing and wordsmithing. But, for my money, none is more important than character development—and in *Carolina's Ring*, Seldon delivers! I wanted to adopt Ben, give Carolina my therapist's phone number, and alternatingly smack and hug the beautifully tortured Alf. If the final scene stays with me forever (as I suspect it will), it's because Seldon is not afraid to depict the yin and yang of human nature."

—Nancy Ritter, Author of *Slack Tide*

"Rivalry between brothers is as old as Cain and Abel, a tension artistically and creatively revived in Lynn Seldon's *Carolina's Ring*, the second book in his planned trilogy. With biblical echoes, one brother is lost and the other found as war and romance combine in a rewarding climax to this fast-paced novel."

—John Warley, Citadel Class of 1967, Author of *Jury of One* and *Stand Forever, Yielding Never: The Citadel in the 21st Century*

"Lynn Seldon's *Carolina's Ring* is a truly engaging book about family, relationships, dreams, and the fragile fibers of love that connect them all."

—Jeffrey Blount, Author of *The Emancipation of Evan Walls*"

"Thoughtful and gripping, Lynn Seldon's newest novel, *Carolina's Ring*, enjoins the reader to a journey of honor, commitment, and lifelong love as the foundation of this compelling story. It is a poignant account offering unexpected turns while commanding one's attention with each turn of the page."

—Pete Masalin, Citadel Class of 1983, Author of *Military Brat* and *The Sorrow of Loss, The Wisdom of Recovery: A Narrative of an Unwanted Journey*

". . . readers settle in to the fast-forward, replay-like sequences and maddening foreshadowing that has them turning pages at lightning speed."

—Rona Simmons, Author of *A Gathering of Men*

"*Carolina's Ring* is an expressive love story cleverly constructed to hold the reader's attention."

—Vice Admiral Sandra Stosz, United States Coast Guard (ret.), Author of *Breaking Ice & Breaking Glass: Leading in Uncharted Waters*

MORE PRAISE FOR LYNN SELDON &
VIRGINIA'S RING

◆

"A triumph and a tour de force. He joins the distinguished ranks of our military academy graduates who have written about the life-changing, fire-tested tribe."

> —Pat Conroy, The Citadel, Class of 1967, Author of *The Lords of Discipline, The Great Santini, The Death of Santini,* and many other bestsellers

"All VMI alumni will smile and nod as they read this. It's a celebration of the many strong ties and emotions that define the VMI experience and a tribute to the sacrifice that is service to our country and our state. A tribute to the seasoning that occurs in all VMI men and women. A must-read for alumni and friends of VMI of all ages."

> —Teddy Gottwald, President of VMI Class of 1983, CEO of NewMarket Corporation

"Lynn Seldon's *Virginia's Ring* will resonate with every man and woman who has stood in the long gray line, eaten a square meal, and sweated at something euphemistically called a party. The man knows his school, VMI, and his love for all he experienced there comes through on every page. This is a story of shared sacrifice, communal values, and unbreakable friendships. It nails academy life, and in doing so summons the best in each of us."

> —John Warley, Citadel Class of 1967, Author of *Jury of One* and *Stand Forever, Yielding Never: The Citadel in the 21st Century*

"In this well-written and accurately portrayed novel, Lynn Seldon shares his love and appreciation for his alma mater and VMI's unique educational experience. The main characters, cadets Nick Adams and Virginia Shields, tell their VMI stories in captivating, moving, and nostalgic reading. This is a fun and must-read for all who wear the ring, and for the entire VMI family."

—Greg Cavallaro, VMI Class of 1984, Former CEO of the VMI Keydet Club

"After I began reading, I was hooked. I could not put the manuscript down. For me, it was much like Pat Conroy's *The Lords of Discipline*. Through his personal knowledge of VMI, Lynn has used his writing talents to weave the Institute's journey with co-education into a very exciting and believable novel."

—Mike Strickler, VMI Class of 1971, and Former Executive Assistant to VMI's Superintendent

"The Virginia Military Institute—it would be hard to imagine a school so influenced by the past as this one, where history and tradition shape personal relationships on a daily basis. Lynn Seldon takes us into this world as only one who has been there can. *Virginia's Ring* reveals the complex and at times conflicted legacy of fellowship and sacrifice inherited by the young men and young women of today. It is a moving story, spanning generations, propelled by characters we come to love."

—Dave Kennedy and Tom Farrell, Writers and Producers of *Field of Lost Shoes*, a feature film about VMI cadets at the Battle of New Market

"This is a book a Southern girl will read in bed, on the piazza, or on the beach."

> —Nathalie Dupree, Co-author of *Mastering the Art of Southern Cooking* and *Southern Biscuits* and Author of *Nathalie Dupree's Southern Memories* and many other books

"Lynn Seldon paints her [Virginia's] portrait with great care, sensitivity, and courage, and in doing so tells us not only her story, but his—he too wears the ring. Death haunts *Virginia's Ring*. It conquers all, but so do family, friendship, and love."

> —Bernie Schein, Author of *Pat Conroy: Our Lifelong Friendship*

"My classmate Lynn Seldon scores big with *Virginia's Ring*. A delight for both alums and those intrigued with the Institute."

> —Wade Branner, VMI Class of 1983, and Veteran "Voice of the Keydets" Broadcaster

Carolina's Ring
by Lynn Seldon

Published by

◄ köehlerbooks™

3705 Shore Drive
Virginia Beach, VA 23455
800-435-4811
www.koehlerbooks.com

CAROLINA'S RING

LYNN SELDON

VIRGINIA BEACH
CAPE CHARLES

"In my mind I'm goin' to Carolina . . ."

James Taylor, "Carolina in My Mind," 1968

With Love to Cele
My Spirit

&

To the Spirit of Pat Conroy
Great Love

PREFACE

WHEN *VIRGINIA'S RING* was originally published in 2014, I could never have imagined the overwhelming positive response from thousands in the "VMI family" and beyond. Originally encouraged by Pat Conroy years earlier, I truly had no idea that my coming-of-age novel would resonate across the ages, with alumni and others, from their teens to their nineties, finding "their" Virginia Military Institute in those pages.

Whether it was signing books in the VMI Bookstore before football games or mailing hundreds of signed and personalized books to people around the world, the last eight-plus years have provided a fulfilling experience that brought my lifelong love-hate relationship with the Institute full circle. It was a true love letter to a special place and singular experience that changed my life.

Carolina's Ring is the second book of The Ring Trilogy, with the third planned title being *Georgia's Ring*. This book is a sequel in some ways, in that characters like Virginia Shields, Nick Adams, and others make return appearances, as do beloved places like Lexington and Richmond. Along with introducing new characters like Carolina, Alf, and Ben, this novel also allowed me to explore two other very special places more closely—The Citadel and Charleston. In many ways, this book is a love letter to the city and the school as well.

Those who have read *Virginia's Ring* will note that several scenes in both books, like VMI's fabled Ratline experience, are told in the same fashion. This was very intentional, in that the many experiences at VMI and The Citadel are quite similar across the decades, and I wanted to relate that similarity in both books.

Though I occasionally deviated to help narrative flow, I worked very hard to handle all referenced historical events, places, and people correctly. Thanks to many VMI and Citadel grads, as well as several Marines, who helped me with this. Any mistakes are completely mine.

Lynn Seldon
Beaufort, South Carolina

PART I

BEN

————◆————

MY NAME IS Ben, and I wear the ring.

My ring holds stories and so do the rings of several other people in my life, including Carolina's. She has several rings that have many tales as well.

I can't remember a time when Carolina wasn't in my life. She was simply always there, long before we earned our various rings in very different ways.

Carolina was with my twin brother, Alf, and me when we played in her big backyard beside our little house, just north of Furman University's bucolic campus north of Greenville and just south of downtown Travelers Rest, my hometown. She was with us on hikes up on nearby Paris Mountain and out on the mile-high swinging bridge at North Carolina's Grandfather Mountain. And Alf and I were with her as teenagers, when we snuck beers below her family's weathered, old, gray beach house down on Edisto Island. As I remember it, Carolina was everywhere we were. Always . . . well, almost.

Alf and I were born in 1981 on Monday, December 7, forty years to the day after that fateful Sunday morning in Pearl Harbor. My mother loved to regale us with the story of how she drove through a rare Upcountry South Carolina snowstorm to Greenville Memorial because Alf—as always—was in a hurry. Starting that day, my mother did so many things for Alf and me, "by my ownself," a phrase she liked to draw out in her sometimes syrupy Southern drawl.

I never knew my father, Jack Marshall. Though he evidently never sped, he died on rain- and ice-slicked State Park Road near Paris Mountain just fifteen days before we were born. He was returning from weekend drill with the South Carolina Army National Guard on a Sunday evening, and Mom says she likes to think he was hustling home to be with her and to see if one of us was still trying to kick our way out into the world. That would have been Alf. My mother says my dad was a very good man in every sense of the word, and no one in our individual or collective lives has ever contradicted that statement.

From the day Dad died, even before we were born, my mother lived and breathed for Alf and me. Except for a small policy that she later told me she'd heard automatically came with serving in the Guard, Dad didn't have any other life insurance. However, my mother somehow made do for us with her office job at Furman. She also supplemented her income by tutoring several of the small and expensive school's scholarship athletes.

My mom was the administrative assistant for Professor Bob Stone, the head of Furman's English department. Like Mr. Stone, Mom was a Travelers Rest native who had returned to town after college.

Carolina was Bob and Sarah Stone's only child, and she was born at Greenville Memorial on the same snowy morning as Alf and me. Mr. Stone drove Carolina's mom to the hospital. We were already there, with a screaming Alf evidently already greeting this sometimes friendly world with flailing open arms. Mom says I came along quietly five minutes after Alf, which was a trend I'd continue.

From that morning forward, I started following in Alf's very wide wake. I was happy to go along for the ride most of the time, and so was Carolina. Alf was always the one who made things happen in our lives—both good and bad. Or at least how we defined good and bad back then.

Thus began our days together, with Sarah Stone calling us "the ABCs" for as long as I can remember, and Carolina occasionally calling me "B" and Alf "A" from the time she started forming letters and words, and sometimes not bothering with our full names once she learned to pronounce them, although she always used our first names when she was angry with one of us, which was rare. I never knew why, but all of us called her Carolina when we were growing up, instead of "C" or even "Car," which we adopted later in due time. We pronounced it, "Care," which seemed appropriate for the most caring person I've ever known.

I know this is true of many twins, and I've even researched it a bit, but Alf and I seemed connected in more ways than just being fraternal—or, as I'd read, dizygotic—twin brothers. We frequently found ourselves thinking the same thoughts and taking similar actions, even when physically separated. Often, our mom or Carolina pointed it out when we both shared something with one or both of them that we'd been pondering or pursuing separately. As we grew into our teens and went off to our chosen colleges, it still happened.

My mother was the first to notice it before we even started school. We would each come into the kitchen late morning after playing in the yard, and she'd ask us what we wanted her to fix us for lunch. At least half the time, we'd say we wanted the same thing. It could be PB and Js and cold milk, or maybe mac and cheese. Or, even more often, it'd be hot dogs smothered in ketchup and mustard, which Alf and I both evidently loved from the time Mom started feeding us solid food. She told us it was our dad's favorite weekend lunch as well.

These coincidences between Alf and me also happened at night, when Mom asked us separately what she could fix us to eat or what TV show we wanted to watch. Of course, the choices were limited back then, so the odds were greater for it to happen. We generally just joked about it when it occurred.

Carolina tells me she remembers first noticing it when we began elementary school together. Unbeknownst to Alf and me, we'd each tell Carolina what we thought about something at Travelers Rest Elementary, like a new teacher, only to discover we had the exact same opinion. This happened with birthday and Christmas presents we requested, baseball cards pursued for specific players, and so much more.

Later, the coincidences at our chosen colleges became even more noteworthy, in that we were physically separated by almost 450 miles, and would only learn later when were back home that it had happened yet again. Sometimes, it was small stuff that just made us all smile. But more than once, like when we chose eerily similar topics for an essay at college, it was obvious that Alf and I were much more than twin blood brothers.

CAROLINA

MY PARENTS ALWAYS called them "the boys," as if they were a single entity, instead of the two very distinct people I grew to know and love. For as long as I can remember, I saw them as two quite unique boys—and then men—that I would care for in very separate and different ways.

Alf and Ben. A and B. I can't recall a single important moment of my childhood that didn't somehow involve all three of us. Until I chose one of them and things between us shifted. And then, years later, there were just two of us. And everything had changed forever.

ALF

— ■ —

I CAN'T REMEMBER a time when Carolina wasn't in my life. She was simply always there. From the South Carolina foothills to Edisto Island, Charleston, and everywhere in between, she was there with me. And us. Always.

At some point, each of us would sometimes call her "Car," as in "Care." It seemed fitting in so many ways.

Many might think that growing up just up the street from Furman University, in the shadow of Paris Mountain, would be idyllic for a boy—and they'd be right. Along with living in the little town of Travelers Rest, we were blessed by South Carolina's foothills nearby and the beloved Blue Ridge Mountains farther to the north, with hiking trails, two- and four-legged wildlife, fish-filled streams, and more of Mother Nature at her best for us to explore. We were also surrounded by friends and my small family, which only a small-town childhood can provide.

We lived on Regent Drive, just a short walk from Furman's pretty campus. Carolina's sprawling backyard next door became our playground as the three of us progressed from playing in a huge sandbox her father built for us to playing house or "Army." Ben and I alternated who played Carolina's husband and son, or she played nurse to our soldiers. I was always an officer, and Ben was an enlisted man, with Carolina consistently splitting her battlefield allegiance to us fifty-fifty.

During one game of Army, I cut my finger on a metal stake
I was using to build a canvas tent I'd found in my dad's National
Guard stuff. After Carolina ran in her house to get some scissors and
bandaging, she came running back to us and said, "Hey, let's become
blood brothers, Ben and Alf!" And we did, with Carolina and Ben
drawing blood from their fingers with the scissors and the three of
us mixing our blood without a word.

BEN

———◆———

I CAN STILL smell the hamburgers Mr. Stone grilled for us on his big, black, Weber charcoal kettle grill in their backyard, back when we were always-hungry teenagers. I can also easily conjure up the Chanel No. 5 perfume that Carolina started wearing the day she turned sixteen down on Edisto Island, when her mother finally allowed her to dab a bit on her long neck. Today, whenever a woman, including Carolina, walks into a room wearing Chanel No. 5, the memories and smells of those days long ago return through my nose to my heart.

The three of us celebrated our sixteenth birthdays with a weekend down at the Stones' long-time family beach house on Edisto Island. The weathered gray house was originally Carolina's paternal grandfather's fishing cabin, and as an only child like Carolina, her father had inherited it when his dad died there in his sleep the winter weekend the three of us were born. Mr. Stone liked to say that life was like that, coming in full circle. I'll never forget that 1997 weekend as long as I live, but not because of Carolina's new perfume.

Edisto Island and the Lowcountry hold almost as many memories of my life with Carolina and her parents as does my time growing up in the South Carolina Upcountry. It was there that I learned about salt water and sand, as I would learn about fresh water and dirt in the mountains. Edisto Island was also where I originally learned about love—and loss.

I first—and some would say finally—told Carolina I was in love with her when we were down on Edisto to celebrate our sixteenth birthdays. Though he hadn't done so very often over the years, Mr. Stone invited our mother to join us for this seminal celebration. It was my mother who I turned to that weekend after I confessed to Carolina I loved her. And Carolina told me she already loved someone else—my brother, Alf.

When I told my mother what happened, she already seemed to know what I hadn't surmised. Her first words hurt me almost as much as Carolina's. Holding my chin up so I could see her tear-filled eyes, she said, "Oh, honey, Alf told me early this morning that he was going to tell Carolina he was in love with her as well." He'd been first to the dance yet again.

From that weekend forward, it would not be the same between the three us. Carolina and Alf both grew apart from me in their own ways, all the while growing closer to each other as our college years approached.

Our school choices, or, in some respects, how our colleges and futures seemed to choose us, would determine our fates together and apart. I chose the Virginia Military Institute in the beautiful Shenandoah Valley. Alf headed to The Citadel in historic Charleston, and Carolina went to UNC in Chapel Hill, a college town in North Carolina's Triangle region I'd grow to love immensely later in life for reasons I never could have predicted.

My mother never could have afforded to pay for Alf and me to attend college, so we knew from a young age that we needed to earn scholarships if we wanted to continue our educations. And with my mom, college was a given. The only college that wasn't on the table for me, Alf, or Carolina was Furman, in that our mom and Mr. and Mrs. Stone had firm beliefs that we needed to go away for college. So we did.

Many may say it was a metaphor for what was to come in my life, but hitting a baseball and running the bases—and stealing them— came easily to me, and I thus received varied baseball scholarship offers from several in-state schools, including partial financial aid options with USC in Columbia and Coastal Carolina near Myrtle Beach.

But our high school baseball coach was good friends with VMI's longtime coach up in Lexington, having sent several players there, so that was good enough for me. VMI chose me, rather than me choosing the Institute. It was the only school where I could get a full baseball scholarship, and I accepted their offer that fall. I thus attended VMI on a full ride, thanks to the support of VMI's fabled Keydet Club and several loyal alums with deep pockets.

For Alf, who excelled at every activity he tried but was never interested in team sports, his march to The Citadel began by earning a four-year scholarship from the Navy, with a Marine Corps officer option that Alf very much hoped and planned to pursue. Hatched in the woods of South Carolina, Alf's dreams of becoming a Marine Corps lieutenant led from Paris Mountain trails down I-26 to Lesesne Gate at The Citadel.

Of course, with her name, Carolina seemed destined to attend either UNC in Chapel Hill or Columbia's USC, which was also simply referred to as "Carolina" when you were in the Palmetto State. Though it was further from Charleston, and Alf, smaller UNC seemed a better fit for Carolina. And it was.

I wouldn't learn until years later, when much had changed, that Carolina chose Chapel Hill because she felt USC would have been too close to Charleston; it would have been too tempting for her and Alf to try to see each other more often than they should. I still find it ironic that Chapel Hill is closer to Lexington, where I was for four long years, than to Charleston—by more than 130 miles. I looked it up.

CAROLINA

I NEVER SERIOUSLY thought of "love" when it came to Ben and Alf until the summer before our sixteenth birthdays back in '97. I'd liked them as my closest friends since I could remember, but love wasn't part of our equation until Alf started treating me differently that summer, just after school ended in May.

By different, I mean that Alf's eyes lingered on my face and my burgeoning woman's body in a way that I'd never previously experienced with him, Ben, or any other boy that I could recall at Travelers Rest High. I'd always been somewhat of a tomboy growing up and never thought much about my looks, but that summer my blond hair filled out, as did my breasts, and even my slate-blue eyes seemed to have a different sparkle when I finally started spending more time looking in the mirror.

That May, my mom told me that I was looking more and more like a young Meryl Streep. Today, when we look at pictures of me back then, we compare my looks more to Streep's daughter, Mamie Gummer, who obviously inherited the acting—and looks—gene from her mom. I'll take the comparisons to either of these pretty women anytime.

Anyway, that June, Alf simply seemed to start focusing more on me instead of Ben, whereas his attention had been divided equally in the many years before that summer. I don't know whether Ben noticed the subtle changes in the way Alf treated me and, if he did, whether he chose to ignore what was happening. I sometimes wonder if Ben deciding to tell me that he was in love with me was some sort of defense mechanism to our trio's changing dynamic.

I'll be the first to say that I liked the changes in the way Alf treated me during that summer many years ago. Looking back, it now seems that the longtime friendship the three of us enjoyed for so long was destined to evolve into something different.

I still truly believe in my heart that if it had been Ben who had started treating me differently, he would have been the one I chose. However, he didn't, and everything began to change that summer, on that crisp and clear December Sunday afternoon on Edisto when I had to tell Ben I couldn't return his love—because I'd already professed my love to Alf. It now seems like nothing was quite as clear for any of us from that day forward.

ALF

———■———

I'M STILL NOT sure I know exactly why I started treating Carolina as more than a close friend that summer, but I guess it was inevitable. She was obviously becoming a woman in front of our eyes, and it was hard not to imagine her being more than a friend for one of us—or someone else—someday. I never asked Ben if he was having the same feelings. I'm not sure it would have changed what happened.

I could tell that Carolina noticed the changes in me and the way I was around her, but we never talked about it then or later. However, her lingering looks and casual touches during the rare times Ben wasn't with us made me realize, or at least hope, that she had similar feelings. In retrospect, I wish I'd told Carolina my feelings for her that summer, instead of waiting until our birthdays weekend down on Edisto. I've always wondered if it would have changed what happened later.

When I told Carolina I loved her that pretty December Sunday morning, I didn't know that Ben would profess the same feelings for her later that day. Carolina never told me, and it wasn't until years later when we were away at school that I learned about it in a short letter from my mother. I never told Ben I knew, but, looking back, my mother's sparse sentences explained and predicted many of the things that occurred after Carolina and I became a couple.

BEN

◆

THE DAY CAROLINA and Alf became a couple was the day our longtime ABCs trio broke up, if it's even possible for three people to "break up" in the traditional sense of the phrase. The chemistry between us was never the same. How could it have been?

The rest of our junior year at Travelers Rest High School was completely different from previous school years, and my heart broke just a bit more each time I saw the two of them walking down the hall hand in hand, or when I knew that Alf was heading next door to Carolina's house to pick her up for a date or an outing with other couples from school.

During that cold winter and damp spring, I became closer than ever to my mother, which hadn't seemed possible back in December. She, of course, knew of loss, and always seemed to know the right thing to say when I was at home without Alf for extended periods for the first time in my life. She also knew when to say nothing at all.

Of course, the summer of 1998 after our junior year was unlike any summer in our short lives as well. The three of us no longer did everything together in that carefree way of teenagers with a full summer ahead of them. All I knew was that Alf and Carolina were enjoying one kind of summer, and I was experiencing loneliness for the first time.

CAROLINA

———————○———————

THAT WINTER AFTER our sixteenth birthdays, and the following spring and summer, came with conflicting emotions. Of course, coming after such a long friendship, my growing love for Alf brought much joy to my life. That was obviously somewhat subdued at times by the hurt I'd caused Ben, and seeing that pain whenever we made now-rare eye contact tempered my generally joyful new life with Alf. I still occasionally notice the same look in Ben's eyes today, but it's now for very different reasons.

I'd known for many years that Alf was interested in the military and service to America, but it really became clear our first summer together as a couple. President George W. Bush said that terrorism was a real threat to our nation's security, and Alf viewed this as another reason to pursue becoming a Marine Corps officer. He never spoke of it as a way to go to college or as a career choice, but more as an obligation—and an honor.

I knew Alf's dear mom couldn't afford for either of the boys to attend college, so both of them, in their own ways, were very focused on scholarships. Ben's talent for hitting a baseball and running the bases got him into VMI, and Alf's passion for the military easily earned him an ROTC scholarship. His first and really only choice was The Citadel. I always meant to ask him if he'd ever considered attending VMI with Ben, which he probably could have with his Navy scholarship. I sometimes wonder if that might have changed what happened.

Once Alf decided to go to The Citadel, my admittedly strange logic provided me with my college choice. I'd heard about girls who dated cadets at The Citadel and went to Charleston whenever they could, which sometimes made it tough for their boyfriends to succeed at a very difficult college.

I didn't want to be one of those girlfriends, so I chose the Carolina that was farther away from The Citadel by 183 miles. I checked. Though I still ended up going down to Charleston a fair amount when Alf was there, and he came up to Chapel Hill a few times, being farther away from Alf proved good practice for what was to come, once Alf entered the Marine Corps.

ALF

———■———

I'D FELT THE Citadel was the right choice from the first time I set foot on campus during a visit to Charleston with my mother and Ben years earlier. We'd driven there for a fall weekend when my brother and I were eleven because my mom wanted to walk the streets where she'd fallen in love with my dad, back when they were students at the College of Charleston.

When we were younger, Ben, Carolina, and I had often played Army in her backyard and out in the woods, with me pretending to be an infantry lieutenant, Ben a private, and Carolina an Army nurse. My mom even outfitted the three of us with Halloween costumes.

Thus, when we went to Charleston, Ben and I both begged Mom to take us to The Citadel for their fabled Friday parade. But it was me, rather than my brother, who fell in love with everything about The Citadel and Charleston that day.

After the parade, which had me in awe from the moment the Corps of Cadets marched onto Summerall Field, we walked around campus, and I found myself constantly looking up at the clean-cut cadets and dreaming of wearing their crisply pressed white pants and gray blouses. Then we drove to downtown proper, where my mom had splurged on a room at Kings Courtyard Inn on King Street.

The front desk manager recommended that we go to Slightly North of Broad over on East Bay Street for dinner. Later, Ben and I began calling the evening meal "supper" because that's the word they'd used at The Citadel and VMI for decades.

That night was the first time I tried shrimp and grits, a dish I would grow to love, along with many other Lowcountry dishes from SNOB's longtime chef, Frank Lee. Mom had steamed shrimp, and Ben ate rabbit for the first time. Mom and I tried it, too.

After a tasty and unique meal—at least for us—we wandered the streets of Charleston, peeking into courtyards with gurgling fountains and simply soaking up the sweet salt air mixed with the conflicting smells of passing horses making their way down cobblestoned streets on popular horse-drawn trolley tours. Our room at Kings Courtyard had two queen beds, and my mother commented that it was the first time Ben and I had slept in the same bed since we were toddlers.

The next morning during breakfast, the same gray-haired woman who didn't seem to leave her post behind the front desk sent us up the adjacent Meeting Street to Jestine's Kitchen for a lunch that I can still taste. It was rare for the three of us to eat out, but when we did go to a restaurant, we each ordered something different, and then shared everything—our family tradition. We'd done so at SNOB the previous night, resulting in three clean plates, and we repeated the food-sharing at Jestine's, with me ordering meatloaf, Ben getting the fried chicken, and Mom choosing a crab cake as the healthiest of our three orders. We also shared a bunch of their famous Southern sides, and I can still taste my first bite of their silky okra gumbo, which I remember Ben hated and spit into his napkin with a grunt.

After lunch, the three of us joined a walking tour of the city that my mom had signed us up for with the hotel. I'd like to say I fell in love with the Holy City that day, but I was honestly too young to appreciate the history, character, and characters. I spent most of the day thinking of The Citadel and telling Mom and Ben that I planned to return to Charleston as a Citadel cadet someday. And I did just that.

PART II

CAROLINA

———o———

I REMEMBER THE fall weekend, when Alf went to Charleston with his Mom and Ben and had his first taste of The Citadel and the rest of the Holy City. It seemed like it was all he talked about that fall and winter with Ben, his mom, and me. His passion for going there did not abate until he reported to campus on a hot and muggy August day in 2000.

When Alf returned from Charleston after his orientation weekend, something seemed changed in him when he came over to our house. My parents were down in Greenville for dinner at a downtown restaurant called Soby's, where Mrs. Marshall had taken me, Alf, and Ben after our sixteenth birthdays. So we had the house to ourselves, which wasn't unusual. What was unusual was that Alf's passionate thoughts about The Citadel seemed to carry over to me as well.

Alf and I made love for the first time that evening, in my bed. It was the first sex for both of us, so I understood the awkwardness, but I got the sense that Alf was checking a box on a list that included sex with me, The Citadel, our marriage, and the Marine Corps. Yes, there was passion and certainly love, but I felt Alf's lovemaking wasn't for the woman I was . . . and am.

Alf's mom drove him back down to Charleston later that August, so I said my goodbyes to him and Ben at their house. I hugged Ben goodbye in their living room, with Alf and their mom sitting nearby. For Alf, our goodbyes took place out on their little front porch, under a single ceiling fan churning up nothing but hot summer air.

As we'd been warned by many alumni and others, we did not hear from Alf for almost two weeks after he matriculated on The Citadel's campus to begin his personal and sometimes very public rites of passage. And then, I only heard from Alf's mother that he had called to say he had survived what they still call Hell Week. From what she could tell from their brief call, he seemed to be doing okay in The Citadel's spartan barracks buildings and beyond.

Though her report on Alf by phone to my dorm in Chapel Hill seemed extensive for my sake, she added that Ben was also fine at VMI, using even more foreign terms like "Ratline" and "dyke," a word that had a very different meaning back then for us, whether in Travelers Rest or up in Chapel Hill.

Alf called me in Chapel Hill twice in September for very short and subdued conversations, where I felt much was left unsaid. When I asked about how his "Knob" year at The Citadel was progressing, he said, "I'll tell you everything when I see you." That never happened that fall.

I didn't see Alf again until late September, when his mom offered to pick me up at Chapel Hill and drive down to Charleston for a weekend visit and football game against Appalachian State, which The Citadel lost 51–0. I was not able to spot him in the sea of white and gray during the Friday-afternoon parade. The first time I laid eyes on Alf as a Citadel cadet was when he found his mom and me on Summerall Field after the parade.

Alf had changed out of his formal parade uniform into a somewhat more casual outfit of shiny black shoes, starched white pants, and a gray blouse with a high black collar that looked totally uncomfortable. He wore a Citadel cap with a shiny shield, but it was easy to see that his hair had been almost completely shaved.

The few females I'd noticed in the parade and now out on Summerall Field also had short haircuts, but not nearly as close to the scalp as Alf's. For some reason, even as Alf started walking toward us with a big smile, I thought of Shannon Faulkner and what I'd heard about her ordeal.

Alf had told me back in the summer that Faulkner was the first female to attend The Citadel, leaving after about a week in the fall of 1995. I'd later learn that novelist Pat Conroy, a Citadel graduate in the class of 1967, had paid for her education elsewhere.

That summer, Alf had also told me about Nancy Mace, the first female to graduate from The Citadel the previous May. The daughter of an Army officer, she was born at fabled Fort Bragg. Mace was eventually elected to the United States Congress in 2020, but—of course—we'll all remember another 2020 election winner, and what followed, much more vividly.

When he reached us, Alf briefly and stiffly hugged his mom and then repeated the same stiff, military-like movements with me. Though Alf was never one for public displays of affection or emotion with me or others, it was the most limp hug I've ever experienced, as if he were trying to hug me without touching me. He seemed somehow shy around us for the first time that I could remember, and, for one of very few times during those years, I felt like an awkward teenager. I can't explain it, but he also seemed somehow a bit shorter, but maybe it was just that he'd lost some weight.

The three of us walked over to one of the benches in front of an imposing building called Mark Clark Hall. While we were walking, I reached for Alf's hand, but he refused to take mine, saying, "No public displays of affection on campus, Carolina. I don't want to get in trouble for what they call PDA here."

Once we got to a bench, Alf sat between us without a word until his mother said with a smile and shoulder nudge, "You look nice in your uniform, son."

He smiled slightly and looked at us both before saying, "Some smart-aleck upperclassman commented on my uniform this morning in formation. Except he yelled it in my left ear and didn't use the word 'nice' in his comments. Can we talk about something other than this place this weekend, Mom?"

And we did just that for the rest of the weekend, and looking back, we pretty much did just that for much of Alf's time at The Citadel. He had several opportunities during that first visit to tell me everything—or anything—about his college experience thus far because his mom left us alone three different times during our short visit. But as he would also be throughout his service in the Marine Corps, Alf was always quite reticent about his time in uniform.

After Alf told us he had to stay in barracks and clean his rifle, Mrs. Marshall and I dined alone that night at a loud and seemingly fun restaurant that had just opened called Hank's Seafood. I wish I could have had fun that night, but I couldn't help thinking about Alf's behavior earlier that day.

I fell asleep back at the Hampton Inn between Meeting and King Streets, wondering what Alf was doing or thinking just a few miles away. I'd learn later from other Citadel men—and women—that it was quite likely he was doing push-ups for an upperclassman that night, and many mornings and nights to follow.

Saturday brought more of the same uncomfortable moments when it was the three of us or just Alf and me. After another parade and awkwardness at the same bench as Friday, Alf had to sit with the Corps of Cadets during the football game, while his mom and I sat with other parents, brothers, sisters, and girlfriends—and a few boyfriends as well, I guess.

After The Citadel's overwhelming loss, Alf seemed quieter than ever. It was almost like the score was indicative of something, but Alf remained quiet, except to tell us that he couldn't join us for dinner that night either. With that, we decided to leave early the next morning for Mrs. Marshall to take me back to Chapel Hill. We said our goodbyes in front of Mark Clark Hall, and I wouldn't see Alf again until Thanksgiving.

Looking back, my first visit to The Citadel was surreal in many ways and so unlike the life I'd enjoyed with Alf before he'd headed to Charleston. He rarely smiled that weekend, which was unusual from a boy who'd crack a smile at almost anything back in Travelers Rest, up in the mountains, down on Edisto Island, and beyond. In Charleston, he only spoke when one of us spoke to him and then said as little as possible, choosing his words very carefully.

Sometimes, when hearing about my experiences in Chapel Hill or his mother's life alone back in Travelers Rest, I saw a glimmer in his eyes that spoke of remembering—and missing—something.

I think he was missing a life he no longer had and knew he could never return to, although I'm only guessing, because the Alf who once had shared everything with me disappeared the day he went to The Citadel and never really returned. I can't find it in my heart to blame The Citadel or the boys who seemed to have changed him in only a month. In my darkest moments—and there were many—I blame Alf for choosing this particular path and marching toward some things I now know were inevitable.

BEN

◆

I REPORTED TO VMI the same day that Alf drove to The Citadel with Mom. She tried for years to be in two places at once for us when Alf and I were apart, which was pretty rare until Carolina chose him, but I made her decision easier by saying I could catch a ride with an upperclassman from Greenville who was heading back to VMI early to help with the "Hell Week" indoctrination of freshmen, who had long been labeled "Rats."

That week, and the six long months to follow as a Rat, changed me in ways I couldn't have predicted. In fact, that August day was the beginning of VMI defining me as a man.

I'd heard all the stories about the difficulty and harshness of the Ratline. The shaved heads. The straining, with our chins tucked into our necks and our shoulders awkwardly pulled backwards, when walking the Ratline in barracks. Upperclassmen yelling at us seemingly nonstop. Eating "square" meals while sitting at attention on the front three inches of our mess hall chairs. The infamous sweat parties and other late-night, middle-of-the-night, and early-morning mental and physical challenges. The lack of sleep. Drum outs for Honor Court violations. All followed by everything else VMI threw at you for the three-plus years after the Ratline ended.

I'd also heard many stories about VMI's storied "dyke" system, an interchangeable term for a Rat and his or her First Class mentor who helped Rats navigate the tricky terrain of that first year. There were also many tales about the post-graduation bond of VMI men and women, who would do practically anything for others who wore the ring—as long as it was honorable. I now know what this bond means in ways large and, seemingly, small.

However, none of this knowledge or the stories I'd heard could have prepared me or others in my class for the accumulation of trials thrown at us day after long day back then. Those first days and nights were just the beginning of a succession of many bad times—and a quite a few good experiences—I can only now truly appreciate.

The litany of VMI's challenges lasted long after breaking out of the Ratline that first year, enduring Third Class sophomore year as a "Rat with a radio," Second Class junior year as a "Rat with a ring," First Class senior year as a "Rat with a Rat," and graduating in a post-9/11 world. All of that due to a decision made by that lost seventeen-year-old boy I used to be. Life—and death—really began for me that summer when I caught the first of many rides to the little town of Lexington, which I'd eventually grow to love.

I didn't know all of this on that bright and hot day and very dark first night, when the thunder and rain were almost as loud as the upperclassmen yelling at me. I just knew I needed to get through that single day and night—and then the next versions of both, whatever they brought.

In a way, back in Travelers Rest before reporting to VMI, I'd learned that life was an accumulation of days and decisions made, and I'd decided I was getting a VMI ring no matter what I had to endure. However, I'd soon learn that getting to wear that ring wasn't as simple as deciding you wanted it. At VMI, like in life, others can manifest an unimaginable destiny for you. And often, you have seemingly no control at all.

I won't go into too many details of my thankfully "normal" Rat year. It's different for everyone, but somehow the same—at least for those who stay. I can't speak for those who left. There were many of them.

Out of 475 or so who arrived on matriculation day, more than 20 left within the week, and dozens more departed in the first two months. Less than 400 made it through the fabled Ratline, and fewer than 225 of us walked across the stage on a sunny May day in 2004.

I stayed at VMI because I wanted to wear the ring back to Travelers Rest—for my mom, for the dad I never knew, for Alf, and even for Carolina. In a way, the great South Carolinian Pat Conroy was also involved with my desire to wear what many consider the hardest-earned ring from a Virginia college.

The summer before Alf and I left Travelers Rest, we both read *The Lords of Discipline*. In words both silky smooth and as hard as nails, Conroy powerfully portrayed life at a military school. For me, it was a love letter of sorts to military schools and the bonds between the men—and now women—who attend them. The book gave me much food for thought, and I'm sure it did for Alf as well, though we never talked about it.

Thinking too much is highly discouraged during your Rat year, and it would sometimes make my VMI experience—and life after VMI—more difficult for me and others. I believe Alf would have said something similar if I'd asked him. I still think too much, and it sometimes comes at a high cost for those who know me, or once knew me.

Although I thought Conroy's book about the system of mental and physical adversity tactics had prepared me for VMI, I should have known that books are often a pale comparison to actual life when you're right in the middle of living it. At VMI, I experienced these tactics firsthand with far from fictional characters.

That hot August, however, the only book that seemed to matter to upperclassmen—and thus Rats—was actually a little booklet called the "Rat Bible," with dozens of pages of information you were required to quickly memorize, or else pay the consequences when you couldn't recite every bit of minutiae in it. I can still recite the names of the ten VMI cadets who died at New Market in May 1864:

Corporal Atwill

Private Haynes

Private Jefferson

Private McDowell

Private Stanard

Sergeant Wheelwright

Sergeant Cabell

Private Crockett

Private Hartsfield

Private Jones

William Henry Cabell (VMI Class of 1865), one of the cadets who was killed, was from Richmond. He's buried at Hollywood Cemetery. I found his gravesite on a hilly run there back in the fall of 2006. Six of the ten soldiers who died at New Market are buried at VMI, in front of a 1903 statue called *Virginia Mourning Her Dead*, which was created by a renowned sculptor named Moses Ezekiel, an 1866 VMI graduate who fought in the Battle of New Market. I'd learn later that Ezekiel was VMI's first Jewish cadet and that he accompanied the coffin of Stonewall Jackson when he was buried in Lexington in 1863. I also learned that he died in his artist's studio in Rome in 1917 and was eventually interred in Arlington National Cemetery.

As I recall all of this, I realize that I erred in calling items in that long-ago Rat Bible "minutiae." That I can still remember the names of those cadets who died in the horrific Civil War surely means something, doesn't it?

ALF

————▪————

I WAS NEVER able to put into words what those first few hours, days, and weeks at The Citadel did to me. I wish I'd been able to. I know my mom and Carolina, and even Ben, tried to get me to talk about it at first, but they finally gave up.

The summer after our respective Rat and Knob years, Ben and I briefly spoke about our similar experiences a few times. But it was only superficial chatter that masked the memories of harsh treatment by boys and girls barely older than us who I'd soon trust my life with on a daily basis in places far beyond the gates of The Citadel.

Any thoughts that the path I'd carved out with my mom, Ben, and Carolina back in the Upcountry would continue were soon erased. From those first trying days forward, I privately marked time with "Before Citadel," BC, and "After Citadel," AC. I found it ironic that the ABC trio of Travelers Rest had become just AC, "Alf and Carolina." And after The Citadel, I'd also mark time with my days before and after becoming a Marine.

That first weekend in late September when my mom and Carolina visited me, I knew I looked and acted like a different person from the one they'd known just a month or so earlier. I tried to talk and smile like nothing had changed, but I knew I would fail from the moment I gave them each an awkward hug that was so unlike the way I normally greeted them, even after a short time apart.

We sat on a bench overlooking Summerall Field in front of Mark

Clark Hall, and I truly didn't know what to say, so I didn't say much. They both looked and acted the same as years past, and I knew I was the one who had changed. I hated the feeling and the way I wasn't responding to their questions beyond just a few curt words, but I just wasn't able to turn back into the old me I'd left in Travelers Rest forever.

I knew I was making both of them uncomfortable and that I should try to verbalize my feelings, explain that it was nothing they had said or done. But I just couldn't find the words. I was already learning that some things were best left unsaid, or at least I thought so at the time. But I'm not sure either my mom or Carolina ever understood that.

I could have eaten dinner with them downtown that night, but I'm embarrassed to admit that I fibbed to them, saying I had to clean my rifle for an inspection. So, the two of them ate downtown on their own. I didn't even ask where they went, which was also unusual for me. I fell asleep wondering if my next four years would be like this, with me being unable to conjure the smiles and words I'd once found so easy.

We had another parade Saturday morning before the football game, and in a surreal repeat of the previous evening, the three of us sat on the same bench and shared nothing but small talk about the weather, Mom's new life in Travelers Rest, Carolina's time thus far in Chapel Hill, and how well Ben seemed to be doing.

I responded to questions when asked, but my mind was racing through everything I needed to complete by Monday morning—from shining my shoes and boots once again to completing my calculus homework. I did get some once-familiar laughs out of both of them when I told them about my calculus homework back in my room, and how barracks would never feel like any sort of home to me.

I had to leave them for lunch formation and then to sit with the Corps of Cadets at the football game, where we were embarrassed by App State. After the crushing loss, which somehow seemed appropriate to my mood, we went back to the snack bar in Mark Clark Hall for Cokes, where I told them that I couldn't join them for dinner that night either. Because they were leaving early the next morning for Mom to take Carolina back to UNC, we said our short and surprisingly curt goodbyes in front of Mark Clark Hall. I wouldn't see either of them again until Thanksgiving break.

I couldn't tell them that I would have given anything to crawl in the back seat of my mom's old, dark-green Subaru wagon and return to what would always be my real home. I know I wasn't the first Citadel Knob or VMI Rat to want to go home during those first few weeks of military school indoctrination. More than a few chose to do so, and I've occasionally thought of tracking some of them down to see if they were glad they left. I always thought it was easier to stay at places like The Citadel and VMI than it was to leave.

CAROLINA

————o————

MY LIFE IN Chapel Hill was so very different from the life Alf had chosen in Charleston. And from Ben's time at VMI as well. I was experiencing what Alf called the "typical" college: freshman year, living on campus, going to UNC football games, exploring sororities, steering clear of other boys and making it very clear I was spoken for, and studying just enough to get the good grades my parents expected, though UNC was most definitely more challenging than TR High. Although I could never claim to know what it was really like for Alf, I felt, in some ways, like I was somehow attending UNC and The Citadel simultaneously.

I once tried to explain this to Alf, and, in a very rare display, he lashed out at me in his own quiet but quite firm and stern way. We were in my dorm room in November, and Alf grabbed my wrist, stared at me, and said, "Nobody, including you, of all people, Carolina, should ever assume that they know what it's like to attend The Citadel unless they are or have. Nobody."

Marine Corps wives claimed that being a Marine's spouse was like being in the Corps. I'm sure Alf would not have agreed with that either, though I never asked.

BEN

◆

I'D LIKE TO say I often thought about Alf—or Carolina—during those first trying days, weeks, and months at VMI, but I rarely did. It was partly because I really didn't have time, but it was also because I'd learned to think less and less about either of them once they became a couple. At least, I tried to think less of losing them, individually and collectively.

My mom was my first VMI visitor during Parents Weekend in October. She drove into Lexington late Friday night after work at Furman, so she didn't check in at the Hampton Inn Col Alto downtown until almost midnight. I thus didn't see her until after the parade Saturday morning. On her way out of town, she bought a bucket of fried chicken from Tommy's Ham House, knowing I'd enjoy a taste of home for my first VMI tailgate with her on the Parade Ground.

After the parade, I quickly changed out of my coatee dress uniform and into my wooly gray blouse with a high black collar, starched white cotton pants with a razor-like crease, and shiny black shoes, which they had me and other Rats shining on a daily basis with a little can of Kiwi. I still use a can of Kiwi on my cordovan Bass loafers today, and the smell of that polish takes me back to my spartan fourth stoop room in barracks.

Upon changing uniforms, which I'd learned to accomplish efficiently and quickly, I made my way in the Ratline down from the fourth stoop to Jackson Arch without being stopped once because all of the upperclassmen were also rushing to get out on the Parade Ground to be with family and friends. As Rats, we had to salute the stark statue of Stonewall Jackson each time we exited Jackson Arch, and after saluting, I saw my mother standing in the tall statue's lengthy shadow.

After a heartfelt hug that both of us allowed to linger, Mom held me at arm's length, smiled, and said, "Nice haircut, Rat, and how the heck did you get even skinnier?" I laughed for what may have been the first time since I'd reported to VMI, and hugged her again. Still with a big smile, my mother looked me over from head to toe in an exaggerated manner.

"I always had a thing for a man in a uniform," she said, smiling. "You have to remember that before you two were born, your father was in the National Guard. I always enjoyed it when he'd put on one of his uniforms once a month for their weekends of what they called 'drill.' He was so good looking."

My mother often told us stuff like this about our father that we hadn't known. "Do you have any pictures of him in his uniform?" I asked.

Her grin faded and she said, "I don't think so. I threw away his National Guard files and all of his uniforms and other stuff when I could finally face going through his closet and the garage more than a year after he died."

"I'm sorry, Mom," I said, taking her hand in mine. "I didn't mean to bring up Dad. I still don't know when it's okay and when it's not."

Her smile quickly returned, and she squeezed my hand and said, "I think I was the one who brought him up with my uniform comment. And you know it's always okay to talk about him, even if it's still hard for me—and the two of you."

"Well, speaking of fathers, I know I can't ever replace Dad, but I want you to meet someone who's become a sort of father figure to me—at least, here at VMI." With that we walked past Jackson's statue to the dozens of tailgate parties already in full force, passing by the smells of grilling meats and the sounds of pop top cans being opened.

About halfway across the Parade Ground, which Rats could only use during parades, tailgates, training, and other rare occasions, my mom asked, "Hey, can we stop by our car to grab my contribution to the tailgate?"

I must admit that the sight of our little Subaru wagon gave me pause; we'd enjoyed so many trips in it. "What do you think about me just jumping in and you taking me home, Mom?" I half joked.

"Oh, you'll want to stay right here, Ben, when you see what I brought from home." My mom dramatically opened the back gate. A bucket of Tommy's Ham House fried chicken brought a smile to my face and memories of my childhood.

"Oh, wow, Mom! This is awesome. I can't wait for my dyke and his parents to try it. Thank you."

My dyke, Brent Dunaway, who—like many VMI cadets and grads—was from Richmond, had invited me and my mom to a big tailgate his family had been hosting since his father attended the Institute. It was actually Brent's grandfather, also a graduate, who started the Dunaway tailgating tradition.

I found Brent exactly where he told me they always set up in the Keydet Club section of the Parade Ground, which I learned later was reserved for big-time donors to VMI's athletic programs. He saw us heading toward their tent and immediately walked over and introduced himself to my mother, holding out his ring-laden hand as he approached.

"Hi, Mrs. Marshall. I'm Brent Dunaway. Welcome to your new VMI family." And with that, he waved his right hand back toward the tailgate, as if revealing a stage set behind a curtain. In a way, it was a stage, and my mom and I were about to become two more actors in the drama.

A bit overwhelmed by the scene, my mother simply gave a quick smile, saying, "Thanks. Please call me Marge. I brought chicken." Brent took the bucket from her, thanked her, and led us over to the crowd of uniformed cadets and a mix of men, women, and other younger people who were likely brothers, sisters, girlfriends, and friends of the cadets.

"Do you normally have this many people, Brent?" I asked, pointing to the crowd as we approached.

"No, this is about twice as many as normal. Parents Weekend brings 'em out of the woodwork, and my father and grandfather put on a party that's even bigger than other football weekends. It's quite the tradition, and now you two are a part of it for life."

Brent walked us over to a group of four men who all held plastic yellow-and-red Keydet Club cups. Each wore a large VMI class ring on their right hands. "Men," said Brent in the assured voice I'd already grown to admire, "I want you to meet the two newest members of our VMI family. This is Ben Marshall and his mother, Marge, from the Upcountry of South Carolina."

Brent then pointed at each of the four men in turn, saying, "That handsome guy is obviously my father, Ted Dunaway, Class of 1955, that's my grandfather, Ed, Class of '33, he's Greg Cavanaugh, also Class of '55, and that's Pat Conaway, a brother Rat of my grandfather there." My mother nodded at each of the men, and I shook their hands as firmly as I could muster.

"It's Coke for you, Ben, but would you like something a little stronger, Mrs. Marshall?" continued Brent. "My grandfather mixes a mean Bloody Mary if you're so inclined."

"No thanks, Brent. But I will take one of those cold Cokes if you have extra."

"Oh, we have extra, Mrs. Marshall. My dad and grandad here bring enough to feed an army, and that's what we usually get at our tailgates. We feed many so-called orphans on football weekends," Brent said, waving his hand at the crowd of cadets from various classes who were gathered around, holding paper plates piled high with food.

"Speaking of feeding, why don't you two grab some chow and meet some more people? You're going to get to know many of them in coming years." With that, Brent wandered off to another group of cadets, two of whom I knew were his roommates. Their plates sagged with burgers and sides.

We spent the next hour talking to alumni, the wives of alums, a few of my new classmates, and a couple of upperclassmen to whom I barely spoke a word out of fear I'd say something that would get me in trouble with them back in barracks. Afterward, my mother asked me about my reticence with upperclassmen, and as best I could, I explained the Ratline and its system of challenges from upperclassmen.

I'll remember that particular tailgate for two specific things. The first, meeting Brent's father and grandfather, Ted and Ed Dunaway, who would take me under their wings at the Institute and beyond, just as Brent already had.

It was also the day I met Virginia Shields.

Dressed in the same uniform I wore and obviously a brother Rat, she walked right up to my mom and me when we were standing alone at the edge of the crowd, holding out her small right hand to my mother and saying, "Hi, I'm Virginia Shields from Richmond."

My mother was unaccustomed to females proffering their hands in greeting but stuck hers out to Virginia's after a second's delay and said, "Hi, Virginia, I'm Marge Marshall. I'm Ben's mom. We're from South Carolina."

Years later, I still recall noticing so many things about Virginia in rapid succession, like a film that has to be rewatched in slow motion to see everything clearly. Here's what I remember most: Virginia looking my mother straight in her eyes and holding her gaze while they shook hands; Virginia repeating the firm handshake and locking eyes with me. And I remember us proceeding to talk as if we'd known each other for years, and it was just her and me on that packed Parade Ground back in 2000.

Virginia was also a Rat, but I hadn't seen her before. Believe me: I would have remembered.

Of course, her blond hair was short, but it didn't make her look like a boy like it did the half dozen girls in my company or the others I'd noticed in my class. The hair beneath her cap escaped out the sides into the cool Lexington air in a way that highlighted her very feminine features. I swear it was the first time in more than six weeks that I'd thought of anything having to do with girls or women—VMI was, and is, a very masculine place. That's true even for the brave girls who go there.

Her hair framed a face that seemed ready to break out in a smile at any time, with mischievous, blouse-gray eyes that were also somehow smiling. Of course, we were in the same uniform, but Virginia seemed to be of another species entirely. I do remember— and I like to remind her—that I thought she looked like the runner she was and is. And, yes, she did—and does—look and act like Carolina in many aspects, from her blond hair to her sparkling, blueish-gray eyes, to her mannerisms and caring ways.

What else do I remember about Virginia that day? Well, she had a confidence in herself that I had not yet mastered at VMI. We immediately started comparing notes about our Ratline experiences thus far, and she seemed to be handling all of the pressures so much more easily than me. She said something my dyke, Brent, often repeated in those first few weeks: "You just can't take it so seriously, Ben."

Brent happened to be walking up to the three of us when Virginia said that and put his arm around me before saying, "See, I told you so, Ben. Listen to your brother Rat here, who seems to be wise beyond her years. Who are you anyway, Rat?"

"I'm Virginia Shields from Richmond, sir."

"There are no sirs out here when we're tailgating, Rat Virginia. I'm just Brent out here."

"Thanks, sir. I mean, Brent."

"So, you're from Richmond, huh? Where'd you go to high school."

"TJ. You?"

"Saint Chris. Once things settle down with the Ratline a bit, let me know through Ben or just come to my room—137—if you ever need a ride to Richmond. I'm pretty much heading there every weekend so far this year."

"That'd be great in a couple of months, sir. Thanks."

"Well, just let me know," Brent said. Then, as quickly as he'd arrived, Brent left the three of us to continue our conversation, though my mom hadn't spoken a word since Virginia had first approached us.

I asked, "Who's your dyke, Virginia?"

"Oh, she's great. Her name is Laura, and she's the one who is giving me the confidence that I can make it through this, get my ring, and graduate. It also helps that I'm running track. That's been a good stress reliever."

"Are you on scholarship, Virginia?" my mom asked.

"Yes ma'am. It's from the Keydet Club."

"So is Ben," said my mom. "He's been a great baseball player since the day I bought him a glove for his eighth birthday. He holds the record for stolen bases back at his high school, and his coach says it'll never be broken."

"Is that so, Ben? We'll have to go for a run one Sunday when we finally have some free time. We'll see how fast you are when you have to run more than sixty feet, or however far it is between bases."

"It's actually ninety feet," I replied, smiling. "And I have pretty good stamina beyond those ninety feet, so I'd love to go for a run with you sometime. But I've forgotten what free time is. Maybe in the spring, if I make it that far."

"What do you mean if you make it, Ben? Of course you will. We both will. Along with not taking things so seriously, Laura keeps telling me to take it a day at a time."

"I keep hearing that 'day at a time' advice, but it's hard to do when you have an upperclassman yelling at you in each ear and another one in your face."

"Oh, don't take it so personally, Ben. Don't let them get to you. And speaking of getting somewhere, we need to head back to barracks for the march down to the football field, don't we?"

And, with that, my life with the fabled VMI family—and Virginia—truly began.

ALF

—■—

THE FALL PROCEEDED pretty much as it had those first weeks before Carolina and my mom had visited. I must admit that I was happy to see them go. I just couldn't bring myself to explain the dramatic changes that were happening in such rapid succession, and I'm not sure it would have done any good to try. The mental and physical pressures remained immense, and the classroom proved almost as difficult for me as life in Padgett-Thomas Barracks and elsewhere on campus. But, like most in my class, I persevered. Of course, some didn't.

The system for essentially forcing some Knobs to leave The Citadel had remained remarkably similar for decades, dating back to Pat Conroy's time there in the mid-1960s—and even earlier, from what older Citadel alums told me. It was essentially a methodical "ganging up" on a Knob by the multitudes with physical and mental stress that very few could withstand. Whether it was for their weight, their inability to perform enough push-ups, or for no reason at all beyond a senior's whim, most of those who were "chosen" that first fall left quickly and quietly, but a few remained and would hold legendary status in our class for going through so much more than most Knobs, which was saying a lot.

Except for one event that forever changed my experience at The Citadel and beyond, my first months at The Citadel were thankfully like those of most of my classmates, with a normal number of challenges that I—rightly or wrongly—internalized. I know from their first visit that my mom and Carolina wanted me to talk about the experiences, but it just wasn't the way I was wired.

The next time I saw them—and Ben—was during our short Thanksgiving break. Though the four of us were together for an early Thanksgiving dinner, I spent most of my time at Carolina's house, either just with her or with her parents as well, who I could tell had been warned by Carolina not to ask about The Citadel.

Whenever Carolina and I were with Ben, it was awkward. There were long pauses in our conversations, and I sorely missed the camaraderie the three of us had once shared. When it was just the two of us over that weekend, Ben and I briefly compared notes about our similar military school experiences. But any chats with Ben had become very superficial compared to those we'd had before Carolina and I became a couple. The only thing I recall from those short conversations was that Ben mentioned a girl named Virginia.

Along with just quietly sitting with Carolina, the other two things I most remember about that Thanksgiving were the two dinners we had. The first was midday at our house, with Carolina coming over to share the meal with Mom, Ben, and me. My mom prepared the traditional turkey and all the fixings, just as she had for as long as I could remember. I didn't participate in much of the conversation, but it still felt very good to eat a meal with three people I knew still loved me—and didn't shout in my ear every other bite like the upperclassmen did at the mess hall.

That night, Carolina and I went over to her house to eat another, very different Thanksgiving meal with Mr. and Mrs. Stone. I most remember the quail that Mr. Stone had shot the previous weekend, grilling them right before we ate. Mrs. Stone had made a bunch of dishes I tried for the first time that day, including brussels sprouts. It was times like this, when I realized how much more worldly Carolina's family and life were than mine, that I sometimes wondered why Carolina had chosen me.

I tried to be my old self for everyone, but it was mostly false enthusiasm, and I'm sure they all knew it. This was especially true for dear Carolina, who I knew was—for the first time in our lives—holding her tongue with me. Looking back, it was another way of showing her love for me and my family. It just didn't feel that way at the time.

The next few days passed relatively quickly, and I found myself looking forward to my return to Charleston. I'm honestly not sure why. That wouldn't always be the case in coming months and years.

I returned to The Citadel that Sunday afternoon, and the march to Christmas began, with my first college exams and many more Knob trials and tribulations dead ahead. I walked back into barracks as determined as ever to prove to everyone in my life that The Citadel had been the correct choice.

CAROLINA

AFTER THAT FIRST September visit with Alf, it was obvious to me and his mother that he was internalizing his experiences at The Citadel, and that asking him about it only made our limited time with him more awkward. Though we thought about returning to Charleston for another football weekend in October, or possibly for Parents Weekend, Mrs. Marshall and I did not return to Charleston that fall. I didn't end up seeing him again until Thanksgiving, when he came home for the long weekend.

Just as he had during our September visit, Alf remained stoic, even when it was just the two of us. It was like his time at The Citadel had made him mute. He did apologize to me about his long silences, and I said I understood. But I really didn't, and honestly never would.

Alf was just as quiet around his mother and poor Ben, who tried to share his seemingly similar experiences at VMI without much success. I became even more aware that Ben might never completely get over me choosing Alf nearly two years earlier. However, I also knew that my choice meant that I must always support Alf, during good and bad times. In retrospect, more bad than good seemed to follow my choice.

Alf returned to The Citadel with his mother late Sunday morning, and Ben and I caught a ride north with a VMI upperclassmen. They dropped me off at my dorm, where Ben gave me a short and awkward hug after saying very little to me from the front seat for the entire four-hour drive to Chapel Hill. I would not see Ben, Alf, or their mom again until the week of Christmas.

BEN

———◆———

MEETING VIRGINIA SAVED me in many ways during my time at VMI, and later. Having her as a brother Rat and, ultimately, much more put the many only-at-VMI tests in perspective that first fall semester, and for years to come.

I didn't actually see Virginia that often; so many of our Rat year activities were based on what company we were assigned to. Virginia was rooming in New Barracks above Marshall Arch with two other girls, and I was in Old Barracks above Washington Arch. Maybe two or three times a week, I would spot her when we were doing something as a class—or Rat Mass, as they called us. At most, we said a quick "Hi" or something. But I knew she was there, somewhere in barracks or on post, and her words the day we met about taking VMI one day at a time resonated with me much more coming from her than from my dyke or my mom.

Brent ended up spending more time with Virginia that fall, winter, and spring than I did because he gave her a ride back to Richmond for Thanksgiving break and continued to take her back and forth throughout our first—and his last—year at the Institute.

Ironically, it was from Brent that I first learned about Virginia's upbringing: her home on Monument Avenue, her deep connections to VMI, and her father, who Brent told me had died of cancer when Virginia was very young. Though I hadn't been alive when my dad died, it provided another bond with Virginia that I didn't share with her for some time.

That first Thanksgiving home from VMI was one I'd like to forget but can't. Though my mom had warned me, it was quickly apparent that my brother was a very different person. During the first four days we'd spent together since leaving for school, I tried without success to share our similar experiences, but Alf's silence tainted the weekend for all of us. I know that it frustrated and hurt Mom and Carolina, and I felt helpless to draw Alf out of The Citadel shell entombing him.

I did mention Virginia to the three of them, but in passing, and it wasn't until Christmas that Carolina reminded me that I'd spoken of her at Thanksgiving. Though I'd learned more about Virginia from my dyke when I returned to VMI in late November, I didn't have much more to share with Carolina or the others over Christmas furlough.

Relatively speaking, when compared with what I'd heard from those at other colleges, I enjoyed the periods at VMI between Thanksgiving and Christmas breaks. The Ratline and, later, other only-at-VMI stuff seemed to take a deep breath as the upperclassmen and administration focused more on exams than on us. Of course, there were still some surprise sweat parties packed with push-ups, sit-ups, and lots of other sweat-inducing exercises, as well as our own seemingly large personal dramas, ranging from the classroom to the daily pressures of the Ratline in general, or sometimes, specifically, when an upperclassman took an "interest" in us.

I saw Virginia only in passing those weeks leading into Christmas. My exams went well, as did Brent's, and again he gave Virginia a ride back to Richmond.

ALF

———■———

CONTRADICTORILY, THE CITADEL felt like some sort of safe haven when I returned from that awkward Thanksgiving back home. It was a place where it was quite acceptable to speak only when spoken to and where stoicism was actually admired, and even praised.

Of course, the pressure on me and my classmates continued, including lots of mental and physical challenges, from memorizing and reciting Citadel minutiae to a plethora of push-ups. And upperclassmen made light of my unique name whenever possible. I'd already learned that you needed to be mentally, morally, physically, and even spiritually tough to make it through The Citadel.

My life back in barracks and in the classroom again defined my existence in the weeks leading up to exams and Christmas furlough. The fact that I remember little of that time is a good thing, in that nothing really bad happened to me, my roommates, or—generally— any Knobs in my company.

I later learned that this was not the case for one female Knob in another company. Like Shannon Faulkner before her back in 1995, this girl had not arrived in August physically prepared for the rigors of Knob year. And just like a handful of my male classmates who came through Lesesne Gate overweight or otherwise not ready for the physical trials, she caught the wrath of upperclassmen in her company, and across campus.

From what I later learned from another female classmate, the targeted girl was determined to stay, despite not being able to complete enough push-ups or successfully navigate obstacle courses and other physical challenges presented to Knobs. This came to a head the week after Thanksgiving.

She returned with a cold, constantly sniffing and blowing her nose, and she refused to go to the hospital. Apparently, it appeared like she was constantly either crying or trying not to, and this just made the pressure from upperclassmen even worse.

She left The Citadel the week after Thanksgiving. I saw her walking across Summerall Field between her parents, her father holding her small duffel bag in one hand and her hand in the other. Later that day, my roommate said he'd heard through the barracks grapevine that her name, ironically, was also Shannon.

In late November, the air turned crisp as a prelude to pleasant South Carolina winters from the Upcountry down to the Lowcountry, which I'd loved since childhood. At The Citadel, on the banks of the Ashley River, the pluff mud smelled different come late fall. For me, the less pungent winter smells were a sign of things to come, before the smell of decay returned in the spring and summer. I always found that ironic because spring was a time of rebirth and new growth rather than decay.

But at The Citadel, I didn't have too much time to think about the smells of Lowcountry pluff mud or pine trees in South Carolina's foothills. I was mostly just thinking about passing calculus, which, unlike Ben, I'd always struggled to grasp. Interestingly, I didn't have a problem with the math required in ROTC for orienteering, which involved the use of a compass, maps, and directions out in the woods outside Charleston.

Late at night, when the sounds in barracks softened to a constant hum, my thoughts ranged from the upperclassmen kicking in our doors before dawn to how I'd treated Carolina the past few months and whenever we were together. I was still just a kid, but I was grappling with fear and love in a way that required a man's experience and fortitude.

But the days and weeks marched forward, and I would thankfully pass all of my exams, including calculus. I always joked with my much smarter brother and Carolina that I'd never be a Rhodes Scholar—I was meant to be a roads scholar instead. I think I was always destined to be a student of roads—roads that led to, rather than away from, enemies near and far.

Christmas came quickly, and I have to admit that, in some ways, I found myself dreading heading back to Travelers Rest. I hated the way I'd become around everyone at home, but it just seemed to be part of how I processed what was happening to me back in Charleston.

Christmas break was much longer, and I saw glimpses of the old me a few times. These fleeting glimmers occurred mostly when I was alone with Carolina on our chilly front porch, or at her house next door. Unlike my mom and Ben, who always seemed to be talking, Carolina was comfortable with silence, just sitting in a swing on our porch or in the worn Adirondack chairs in her backyard without saying a word. As it had always been for the three of us growing up, we never let winter get in the way of being outside in and around Travelers Rest. Just the two of us now, we put on more layers and, when we were over at Carolina's house, lit a fire in the large and weathered stone pit her dad had built years ago.

I'd say there were words spoken less than half the time we sat together, and those conversations, if you'd call them that, felt awkward and stilted compared to our earlier years together. I just couldn't put into words what was happening in Charleston. At least not then.

But Carolina was there, as always. She'd hold my hand and stare off into the distance, occasionally remarking on a winter cardinal's call or sighting. When we were kids and we were the ABCs, cardinals were our bird. It's funny, I don't remember ever seeing a cardinal in my entire time at The Citadel. I always meant to ask Ben if he saw them up in Virginia.

CAROLINA

———●———

THAT FIRST CHRISTMAS break back from Chapel Hill felt like
an extension of Thanksgiving in ways. Alf remained as stoic as ever,
despite my subtle efforts to draw him out and back to me—and us.
After so many years of never having a single awkward moment or
discussion with him or Ben, our days and nights were filled with
difficult quiet hours.

Looking back, Thanksgiving and Christmas somehow brought
me back to Ben on several levels. Along with their mom, Ben and I
shared a feeling of helplessness when it came to our Alf. He spent
more time alone in his room than ever before, and that often left Ben
and me together, with and without their mom, whenever I was over
at their house, which was still often.

At first, Ben and I mostly talked about our college experiences. I
told him everything about Chapel Hill and how much I was loving it
on campus and in the classroom, but also rushing for Tri Sig sorority
and working a few hours a week with UNC's daily newspaper, *The
Daily Tar Heel*.

Carolina alum Charles Kuralt, my idol from the time I began
falling in love with the written and spoken word, had worked at the
paper as well, and eventually became the editor his senior year at
Carolina in the mid-1950s. Kuralt spoke at Kenan Stadium in 1993
to celebrate the school's 225th anniversary, saying, "What is it that
binds us to this place as to no other? It is not the well or the bell or the

stone walls. Or the crisp October nights or the memory of dogwoods blooming. No, our love for this place is based on the fact that it is, as it was meant to be, the university of the people."

The Charles Kuralt Learning Center opened to people like me in May of my freshman year. During my sophomore year, I would go to the Center to research a paper about Kuralt's travels. I even started hanging out at Carolina Coffee Shop on Franklin Street, which I'd heard was one of Kuralt's favorite haunts when he was a student. Kuralt's brother, Wallace, had owned an independent bookstore on Franklin called the Intimate Bookshop for more than three decades, until it closed in 1998. I know I would have loved it.

I even volunteered at the Center during my final two years at Carolina, as well as helping a Kuralt expert, Ralph Grizzle, who was putting together two books about Kuralt. I still have those books in the little bedroom library I've added to since childhood. They were *Remembering Charles Kuralt*, a collection of narratives and anecdotes, which Mr. Grizzle (I didn't call him Ralph back then) published in 2001, and *Charles Kuralt's People*, which he compiled, edited, and published the following year. It was also a wonderful compendium of varied stories written by Kuralt, which focused on the unique characters he'd met out on the road.

In the other book, Grizzle included a great quote from a Kuralt interview in 1994: "It really is rewarding to keep your eyes open and permit yourself to be detoured. I understand that people want to have as many experiences as they can crowd into whatever time they have. It's the condensation of time. We all have so little of it."

Years later, I came across a somewhat similar quote from the South Carolina writer Pat Conroy, whom both Ben and Alf loved. In *My Reading Life*, Conroy had asked, "Why do they not teach you that time is a finger snap and an eye blink, and that you should not allow a moment to pass you by without taking joyous note of it, not wasting a single moment?"

Back in TR over Christmas, during a quick talk alone with Ben, he told me about some of what he referred to as transformative experiences and trials at VMI. Likely for my sake, he compared them to what Alf was facing, perhaps as an explanation for the way he had been treating me, and us. Looking back, I realize that this tied Ben and me together in a way we'd never been before, and that it started to heal the wounds between us that I always blamed myself for causing.

Ben seemed to be handling VMI so differently—and better—than Alf at The Citadel. I asked him about this, and he said Alf might be thinking about what was happening too much. Ben said he'd quickly learned that thinking about things too deeply at VMI wasted time and energy, as well as being depressing.

He also told me that, though it was difficult, I shouldn't take Alf's moodiness and silence personally. Ben felt that Alf would adapt and start handling the pressures of military college better. When I asked Ben what he thought would happen if Alf kept bottling up everything inside, he thought for a long time before saying, "He can't keep it all inside. Something will burst."

BEN

———◆———

THOUGH I WAS grateful to return to TR for Christmas furlough, my enjoyment of virtually unlimited and relatively stress-free meals and sleep for three weeks was again clouded by Alf's general silence. On the drive home and before we picked up Carolina in Chapel Hill, I asked Matt, the First-Classman who was giving us both rides to and from the Upcountry, what he thought about Alf's reaction to his first year at The Citadel.

"I had a roommate like that back in my Rat year in '97," he replied, looking straight ahead as we sped down I-81. "He seemed so stoic about everything and just went about his business without much interaction with us, his roommates, or other brother Rats. I kind of admired him the first few months, but looking back, he was like a tea kettle that was too full and would eventually boil over.

"Then, just after we returned from Thanksgiving furlough, some Third-Classman—I can't remember his name—stopped him in the Ratline and started grilling him about all that VMI history we were supposed to memorize from the Rat Bible. I was right behind him, and he seemed to be handling it like he always had since August, but the next thing I knew, he punched the guy in the gut and marched off to our room ahead of me, out of the Ratline, like he owned the place."

"Wow. What happened to him?" I asked, naturally thinking of Alf back at The Citadel.

"By the time I got back to the room, he was already throwing stuff in his green duffel bag. He walked out of our room in less than ten minutes, leaving his uniforms and everything else related to VMI behind. If Thirds had been allowed up on fourth stoop, you can bet the guy he'd hit would have come barreling into our room.

"Of course, we never saw him again, and I honestly have no idea where he is now. His dyke came by our room about an hour later and told us his girlfriend had broken up with him Thanksgiving Day. Nine times out of ten, Rat, it's something to do with a girl," he joked, never taking his eyes off the road.

We picked up Carolina in front of her UNC dorm and, unlike the drive back north after Thanksgiving break, I tried being more talkative. Though I knew it might worry her, I shared the story the upperclassmen had told me but ended the tale with a smile to keep the mood light. "So, the moral of this story is that you shouldn't break up with Alf on Christmas Day!" That made Matt laugh and glance in his rearview mirror for Carolina's reaction.

She laughed half-heartedly and replied, "Don't worry, guys. I'm in this for the long haul, like those military wives Alf told me about before he went to The Citadel. It's almost like they join the Marine Corps as well, right?"

I hesitated before responding and even glanced at Matt to see if he was going to say something, then turned back to Carolina and said, "I've heard that's the case, and my Army ROTC advisor said it was like that for his wife when they were stationed nine different places around the world during his first twenty years in the Army. He's a VMI grad, and this is his last assignment before he retires back in Lexington. Maybe you and Alf will do the same and end up down in Charleston or something."

"I think I'd like that. The time I've spent there so far has been great, though I have to say my time at The Citadel wasn't nearly as fun as the rest of my time in town. Alf's a very different person from the one you and I grew up with, you know?"

"Believe me, I know," I replied, turning around again to look her in the eyes and emphasize how much I agreed with her. I hesitated before continuing, holding her gaze as best I could, saying, "I'm not sure I wouldn't be the same if I had a girlfriend and she visited me at VMI."

Before she replied, I couldn't help but wonder if Carolina was thinking the same thing as me, that she could have easily been the girlfriend coming to VMI to see me instead of going to Charleston to be with my now aloof brother. Holding my gaze, she said, "Well, I'm sure you'll have a girlfriend visiting you soon enough, Ben, and we'll just see how you treat her. I'm betting you won't be like Alf when it happens. Hey, what about that girl Virginia you mentioned at Thanksgiving?"

I tried to deflect the question by turning back toward the road and asking Matt if he'd run across a female Rat from Richmond named Virginia, but he quickly said no and fell silent. Carolina filled the pregnant pause by tapping on my shoulder and mischievously asking, "So, what about her, Ben?"

Though I felt my face flushing, I turned back to her and said, "I honestly haven't seen her much at all. She's in a different company and way over in New Barracks, plus she's majoring in English, like you, Carolina, so it's unlikely I'll run across her much."

"Well, you sure do know a lot about her for not seeing her much at all, Ben," she said, smiling in that mocking way that I loved and hated in equal measures. "What does she look like?"

"She has short hair," I quickly responded, hoping that I could change the direction of the conversation. What I failed to say was that Virginia looked a lot like Carolina would have with her hair cut short.

"Well, is she pretty?"

"I guess so," I said, facing the road again in another attempt to end her line of questioning. "It's a little hard to tell, exactly, in our uniforms."

"Well, I'd love to meet her sometime when your mom and I—and maybe Alf—come to Lexington."

"We'll see. Who knows? She may not even come back to VMI

after Christmas furlough. My dyke says dozens of Rats don't return."

"Have you ever thought of leaving, Ben?"

With a First sitting next to me, it was really hard to tell Carolina what I longed to say. Instead, I simply said, "No. I'm going back in January. It's not that bad."

At that, Matt spoke for just the second time since we'd picked up Carolina. "It's going to get worse come January and February before it gets better. Thirds hate coming back after Christmas too, and they tend to take it out on Rats."

I didn't respond, but—of course—Carolina continued with her questioning by asking, "Is it harder on the guys or the girls at VMI, Matt?"

He looked at Carolina in the rearview mirror for what I thought was a bit too long before responding. "I really can't say. I haven't had too much contact with the few females who have come to VMI so far." Again, he stared at Carolina using the mirror before continuing with, "I've always felt that, whatever the sex, or lack thereof when it comes to barracks, it's all about how the individual deals with the daily pressures on post, whether they're a guy or girl."

With that, his eyes returned to the road, and he didn't say another word until he pulled up to my house. He offered to drive Carolina next door, but she quickly declined and got out with me.

We walked into our house together to find Alf and Mom sitting in the living room. "Hey y'all," I said, closing the front door behind us. "When did you get home, Alf? And thanks for baking those chocolate chip cookies just for me, Mom."

"About an hour ago, and I've already eaten three of 'em, Ben. And you know she baked them just for me, as always. I was just telling Mom that I think I passed all of my classes, though two of 'em by a thread. I'm just hoping I don't have to retake anything. It's hard enough at that place without getting behind on grades and credits."

"I know what you mean, bro. I think I passed everything too. Of course, Carolina probably got all A-pluses or whatever, yet again, just like at TR High."

"Chapel Hill isn't exactly high school, y'all. There are definitely going to be some Bs or Cs in my UNC future. I think it seems appropriate that an original member of the famed ABCs gets all of those grades, don't y'all?" she asked, smiling.

"Oh, woe is you," I laughed. "Poor little B and C student."

"There are some seriously smart students in the English Department, and we can't all get As," she replied with a slight defensiveness I'd rarely heard in her voice.

"Oh, you know I'm just kidding, smart girl," I said. "But I can promise you that Alf and I don't have quite the academic competition you do, do we, Alf?"

"Nope. I was just telling Mom that if they gave out grades for spit-shined shoes and boots and rifle marksmanship, I'd be a Rhodes Scholar by now. My shoes and my M-14 aren't nearly as complicated as calc equations."

"I hear that, Alf," I said.

"Speaking of hearing something, Alf and Mrs. Marshall. Have you heard that our Ben here has a girlfriend?"

I jerked my head back toward a smirking Carolina and quickly retorted, "Like hell I do, Carolina! And excuse my French, Mom—which I passed, by the way. Carolina doesn't know what she's talking about."

She ignored me and continued her story as if she were a reporter on the nightly news, saying with a smile, "Her name's Virginia, she's from Richmond, and Ben just doesn't know she's his girlfriend yet. But I hear she's cute in a uniform."

"Ignore her, you two. She's totally making this up."

"I remember her," said my mom, staring at me with the same grin as Carolina. "She was really cute. And she seemed so put together, given the circumstances. I'm sure VMI is even harder on girls."

"I don't know about that," I said, sounding as defensive as Carolina had about her grades earlier. "I kinda feel like VMI is as hard as you make it. Is The Citadel that way, Alf?"

After a long pause that had the three of us wondering if he was going to respond at all, Alf quietly said, "Maybe. I sure know I seem to be making it hard on myself sometimes."

"What do you mean?" asked Carolina, who was obviously trying to get Alf to open up about The Citadel. "Are you getting in some sort of trouble there that makes it hard?"

He paused and looked out the window as if he were looking back toward Charleston, then said, "No, it's kind of just the opposite. I think and work so hard at staying out of trouble, after some initial issues I had, that I get all worked up. And it seems almost as bad as getting in trouble in the first place."

"You're most definitely thinking too much, bro," I said, trying to catch his drifting eyes while keeping the conversation light. "You just have to go with the flow under all that pressure, most of which is just nonsense."

"I know, I know, Ben. My ROTC advisor and everyone else says I'm taking it all too seriously, but I just can't seem to help it."

Then, my mother, who—as far as I knew—had only addressed Alf's stoicism with me and Carolina, said, "Well, it's going to drive you crazy if you keep taking everything so literally, and then keep it bottled up inside. I can't believe this is the first time we've really talked about it, Alf."

"I know, Mom," said Alf. "They sort of teach us to suck it up, as far as expressing our feelings, but I guess I've taken that too far. I just don't know how to stop worrying about everything so much."

"You should do like my dyke does and I'm trying to do as well, Alf," I said, still unable to lock eyes with him to drive home my point. "He says to worry about the classroom stuff and that life in barracks and in the Ratline will take care of itself. That seems like great advice for a lowly Knob like you, too," I said.

"That's what I've heard about UNC as well, y'all," said Carolina. "Focus on the classroom, and everything else will fall into place."

At that comment, Alf jerked his neck to stare at Carolina beside him and, with words that were more of a command than a request, said, "Don't you ever, ever, compare your life at your little college to what I'm going through at The Citadel, Carolina. Never!"

Alf kept his icy stare on Carolina, and after pausing, she simply looked down at her hands in her lap. The three of us remained quiet and in shock for what seemed like minutes but was likely only a few seconds. Alf seemed to come out of his trance and grabbed Carolina's trembling hands with both of his. "I'm so sorry, Car. It just came out of me before I could stop it."

After a long pause, Alf quietly continued, "This is no excuse to you, Car, or you two either, but the College of Charleston guy I caught a ride home with said something similar about academics and fraternities at the so-called College of Knowledge, and I barely held my tongue. Except for maybe Ben and others attending military colleges, as well as military school alumni, I'm just not sure y'all understand how different and hard The Citadel is."

"But aren't you making it harder, son?" my mom asked.

"I know I am," he said, finally looking her in the eyes as well. "I just don't know how to stop."

I tried again to catch his eyes and said, "My dyke says that not taking everything so literally or seriously gets easier week by week, month by month, and year by year, but that everyone is different in how long—or short—that process is."

"Well, at the rate I'm going, I think we're talking a year," said Alf, showing a glimmer of the smile and humor we'd not seen since August. "But they're not going to break me."

"It doesn't sound like they're trying to," I responded, trying to keep the tone light. "From what you've said—and that's been very little, Mr. Stoic—you're not getting treated any worse than the other Knobs."

Alf hesitated before replying. "That's somewhat but not completely true, Ben, and I keep telling myself that when they're yelling at me, but I just seem to let it get to me more than my roommates and most of my other classmates."

"I have a roommate at VMI who's more like you, and I'm not sure he's coming back after Christmas," I said.

Alf then snapped his head toward me, finally locked eyes with mine, and said in an almost animal-like voice, "Oh, I'm going back after Christmas, Ben. That's a guarantee to all three of you."

"I'm sorry. I didn't mean to say or imply otherwise. I was really just telling you that my roommate was letting the place get to him too much and that he might not return."

"I got what you were saying, Ben. I got what you all were saying. Let's not talk about it anymore. Or ever again." He got up from the couch and walked to the kitchen where, in the silence that followed in his wake, we heard him open a cabinet, get out a glass, and turn on the faucet.

Until he went to The Citadel, my brother would have always yelled back to the living room and asked everyone if they also wanted something to drink. However, the only sound that came out of the kitchen this time was the sound of running water. To me, the gushing water sounded like someone or something trying to navigate away from us down a rushing river or even a towering waterfall. Whether it was to fill a glass half or all the way full or to let it run down the drain, only time would tell.

ALF

———■———

FOR CAROLINA TO compare her experiences in Chapel Hill to mine at The Citadel may have been the single most ignorant thing I'd ever heard her say to me or anyone else, but that wasn't saying much. Carolina was the smartest, kindest person in words and actions that I'd ever known, and she very rarely had a bad thing to say about a person or situation.

Of course, I immediately knew I shouldn't have snapped at Carolina or my mom and Ben, but I'd just been keeping way too much of it inside for much too long. The past four months felt like four years, and I had no idea how I was going to make it to my final year at The Citadel, when I'd earn my ring in November and my diploma come May.

My silence and moods mostly concerned a single event at The Citadel. Although I knew I wasn't being fair or truthful, I planned never to share it, or other difficult experiences, with any of them. And I knew they were all just trying to help, in their own ways, but I couldn't seem to act otherwise. I'd always been the life and laughter of the party, but the strain of what had happened back in the fall, and Citadel life in general, had replaced that life and laughter with my so-called stoicism.

Without thinking about it much when we were growing up, I started to realize that all three of them had taken my happiness and success for granted. Now my behavior the last four months had disappointed the three people who cared most about me, and I was letting myself down, which only added to my struggles.

After my regretful treatment of Carolina and abrupt departure from the living room, I simply stood at the kitchen counter, gazed out the window into our little backyard through teary eyes, and gulped down a glass of water. It didn't seem to cleanse my body, my mind, or my thirst for perspective when it came to The Citadel and those I loved.

It was Mom who came into the kitchen just a few minutes after I'd left them in the living room. She approached me from behind after I set the glass down on the worn and faded tan linoleum counter, hugging me around the waist and placing her cheek on my shoulder.

"My poor little son. For the first time I can remember, none of us knows what to do, Alf. Help us."

"Don't you think I want to, Mom? I lie awake in my little bed back in barracks and wonder why I can't be like most of the other Knobs and upperclassmen. Or Ben. I just take it all way too personally and I can't seem to shake this ever-present fear of something going very wrong down there. Like having to leave The Citadel. Or losing my scholarship. It's worse at night, when the voices of barracks and my way too active brain keep me awake. And sleep is a precious thing for Knobs right now."

"I know, I know, Alf. I just wish there was something—anything— we could do. Would you maybe like to take next semester off and just take some classes at Greenville Tech or something to see if that's a better fit for you?"

This time, I tried to keep my anger and words in check, glad that she was behind me and I didn't have to see her worried face. "I told you, Mom, that I'm not leaving The Citadel until I'm wearing a ring on my finger and I have a diploma in my hand. Am I clear?"

"Yes sir," she replied, and I felt her smile on my shoulder. "Well, you know we're here for you. Always."

"Thanks, Mom," I replied. "And I apologize if I've let any of you down this past four months. And I'm really sorry how I just treated Carolina. I try to leave this all behind in Charleston when I come home. And especially now at Christmas."

"Oh, don't worry about that, Alf. Carolina—and all of us—are with you through thick and thin."

With that, I turned to face her and, with a long hug, said into her shoulder, "Thanks for everything. I love you, Mom."

CAROLINA

WHEN ALF SNAPPED at me over Christmas break, it gave me a chill that I'll never forget. Looking back, it was the first of just three times I'd have that feeling.

There was a steeliness to Alf's words and cold-hearted stare that I'd never seen. I had silently looked away, which, until that time, was an unusual response for me. Silence and not facing up to people and fears were not traits I liked to see in myself or others.

Though no words were spoken once Alf left the living room, the three of us seemed to know that it was best for Mrs. Marshall to go to the kitchen to console Alf. Ben and I retreated to their chilly front porch but couldn't bring ourselves to discuss what had occurred. After a few minutes, I simply said I thought I should head home.

In retrospect, leaving their house seems awful and uncaring to me. I think we were still all stunned by Alf's words, as if we had broken some sort of dam to Alf's feelings and we were all terrified.

My house was just a hundred feet or so from the Marshalls' but felt a world away at that moment. It felt good to walk the street of my childhood, where the three of us had learned to ride bikes and navigate what we thought were difficult times in our teens. Actually, until Alf had reported to The Citadel, the only truly tough time for me had occurred when I'd chosen Alf over Ben, changing our idyllic teen years forever.

Although my house was quiet when I entered through the

kitchen door, it was alive with the smell of oatmeal cookies—my favorite—that must have just come out of the oven. I spied them on the gleaming black-and-white granite counter, and when the screen door slammed behind me, my mother yelled from somewhere upstairs, "Welcome home, Carolina!"

Then, from his book-lined office just down the hall my father shouted, "Hey, little girl!"

I next heard my mother's quick, muffled footsteps on the front stairs runner and my dad's slippered feet in the hallway. Mom followed him through the kitchen's open doorway as I crossed the tile floor to meet them and they engulfed me in a hug.

"Welcome home, baby girl," my mom said, stepping back to hold me at arm's length while Dad stood beside her and they both just smiled and stared. "We missed you."

"I just saw y'all about three weeks ago." I smiled back at them. "You couldn't have missed me that much."

"The house still feels so empty without you, Car," said my father, still staring at me if I'd just returned from China instead of Chapel Hill.

"How was your trip back?" Mom asked.

"It was pretty good until I got here," I said, looking back and forth between them before continuing. "I had a great talk with Ben and the same VMI cadet who gave us a ride at Thanksgiving, and they both gave me some things to think about with Alf and what he's going through at The Citadel. But then, Ben and I went into their house to see Alf and Mrs. Marshall, and I said something that really angered Alf."

"What in the world could that have been?" asked my dad. "I can't think of a single time in your life that you've ever said or done anything that upset that boy. Or Ben or Marge either, for that matter."

"I know, I know," I responded, communicating my distress to both of them with my tone and tear-filled eyes. "I just tried to compare what I was experiencing at Chapel Hill—balancing classes, rushing Tri Sig, and working at the paper—with what Alf was going through with academics and the military at The Citadel. He sorta snapped at me. No, he definitely snapped at me."

"Hmmm," my father responded, lost in thought. After a few seconds of staring into my eyes, he said, "Given what little I know of military schools and—of course, sororities—I'm afraid that wasn't a wise comparison for you to try to make."

I couldn't hold his gaze after this seeming criticism and looked to my mom for support, but she was already nodding in agreement with my father.

And that's when I finally broke down and fell back into her arms. My father then embraced us both and said softly into my ear, "If that's the biggest mistake you make in your relationship with Alf, I think you'll be okay, Car. He's obviously just very sensitive right now about what he's going through."

"I keep telling myself that," I said into my mother's shoulder. "He's just not making it very easy for me or any of us to try to help him get through this."

"Alf's not the first or last person to struggle with the challenges of college, especially somewhere like The Citadel. But he's a strong young man, and your mom and I believe he'll work through this. You two will be an even better and stronger couple once he does."

"Do you really think so? I've never told Alf or anyone else, but I lie awake at night in Chapel Hill, wondering if we're going to be able to get past this. He just seems so wounded right now."

"I know this may be hard to hear," my mom said, "but if Alf's not able to work through his struggles down in Charleston and the ones he's evidently brought back here, then your long-developing relationship with him won't work out either."

"That's exactly what keeps me up at night, Mom. Do you think that could happen?" I asked, stepping back from the two of them and taking a hand from each.

After looking at my mom, my father took my chin in his free hand and said, "Your mother and I were just talking about this over coffee this morning, wondering if Alf's struggles would have changed since Thanksgiving, when you first told us he seemed to be having issues there. Well, we were hoping as much as wondering. Evidently not. But we both felt that he was going to eventually work through it and that you two would come out an even better couple on the other side. You know we love that boy next door. Well, both boys next door."

"I hope you're right, Dad," I replied, still grasping their hands in the hope that they could pass some of their confidence to me. Trying to lighten the mood, I added, "Do you mind telling Alf the same thing?"

Dad blurted the laugh I loved and missed before saying, "I just might do that, Carolina, I might just do that." I'd learn much later that my dear dad did just that.

BEN

◆

THOUGH I'D HOPED it would be otherwise, it was immediately apparent the first day home for Christmas furlough that my brother was still struggling with The Citadel. I began to believe that something—or someone—had specifically caused his reticence and moodiness. If that was the case, he needed to let somebody else know sooner rather than later.

After his outburst at Carolina, it seemed we'd all decided once again not to bring up The Citadel in Alf's presence. This generally meant that we didn't talk about VMI or UNC either, which limited our topics of conversation the entire time we were home for Christmas.

Alf did seem to return to his old pre-Citadel self when we talked about home, and he perked up most when we reminisced about our time together growing up, back when it was the three of us instead of them as a couple—and me.

I wasn't sure at the time if he longed for those more innocent years, or if he was possibly regretting his commitment to Carolina—and to The Citadel and the Marine Corps as well, actually. All of these choices were made as a teenaged boy. I couldn't help but wonder if he simply felt overwhelmed by the enormity and unknown nature of these decisions and if it was somehow clouding his short- and long-term vision down in Charleston. Looking back, I wish I'd asked him about this over Christmas. Maybe things could have turned out differently.

ALF

———■———

THE REST OF Christmas break came and went, though its length made the silences between me and Carolina and everyone else in my orbit even more unbearable for all of us. In a weird way, I couldn't help but look forward to returning to The Citadel, where I was told what to do and I did it. Mom, Ben, and Carolina kept believing and saying that I was the one thinking things to death, but they were wrong in most ways.

After I returned to Charleston following Christmas break and my failure to improve my attitude, which was mostly internalized, I found myself practically reveling in the sameness of weekday days and nights at The Citadel. From reveille to taps, and with a few only-at-The Citadel exceptions, each day marched forth with me generally knowing what was coming next, minute by minute and hour by hour. And I found that I liked it.

CAROLINA

THOUGH I HATED to admit it, I was ready to go back to Chapel Hill a week before I was scheduled to return. I found that Alf's long silences not only stressed our relationship but also tainted my time with everyone else back in TR as well, including Ben, Mrs. Marshall, my parents, and even my few friends from town. For the first time in my life, I found myself wishing I'd developed tighter bonds with other people at home. Those much-desired friendships were quickly happening at UNC

Besides the episode with Alf in their living room, the other thing I remember most about that Christmas was a story Mrs. Marshall shared with all of us.

For as long as I can remember, I'd spent Christmas morning with my parents, opening presents and eating homemade cinnamon rolls. Then, about ten, I'd walk over to the Marshalls' house and we'd exchange presents, before having what Mrs. Marshall called "Christmas smörgåsbord and s'mores," when, along with traditional Swedish smörgåsbord foods like sliced ham and other cold cuts, plus pickles, smoked fish, and Swedish apple cake for dessert, she'd light an already-prepared wood fire in the backyard, and we'd make s'mores during what was typically a cold Christmas day. Mrs. Marshall had established many memorable traditions like this one, and many of them were masculine in a sense, perhaps to make up for the general lack of a father figure in the lives of her sons.

We were toasting marshmallows over a smoky fire, and I asked, "How'd you come up with this idea, Mrs. Marshall?"

"I'll answer that in a sec, Car, but I keep meaning to tell you that I'd love for you to finally start calling me Marge. All my friends do, even though it's officially Margaret."

I was blowing on my marshmallow while looking at her, and I remember thinking that this woman, Alf and Ben's mom, had truly become my friend. I held my eyes on hers before smiling back and responding, "I'd love that, Mrs . . . umm, Marge."

"Good. Now that that's settled, I'll tell you about the marshmallows. And then I have another story for you three musketeers.

"Okay, first comes the Christmas marshmallows story. Well, actually, the so-called Christmas smörgåsbord tradition came first. The boys know—and you may too, Carolina—that my mother, their grandmother, was of Swedish heritage. She was born in the United States, but her parents emigrated from Sweden in the 1940s during World War II. Though we never did anything like it when I was a kid because my father liked his Southern cooking, my mom sometimes regaled me with stories about their Swedish-style Christmas dinners growing up.

"As you know," she continued, catching Alf's eye, "Alf here is named for his maternal grandfather, who was officially named Alvar but went by Alf from birth, just like our Alf. Well, after my mom passed away, when Ben and Alf were still in diapers, I came up with the whole smörgåsbord thing as a sort of homage to her, her parents, and their temporarily lost Swedish traditions.

"The s'mores idea came a few years later when I decided to try grilling hot dogs for the feast because neither of these boys would eat the huge ham I always bought. When I went to get the hot dog buns out of the cupboard, I saw the marshmallows and said, out loud, 'Voilà, let's make s'mores!'"

Smiling at the long-ago memory, she continued. "We grilled hot dogs and marshmallows over a charcoal grill those first ten years or so, and then we switched to building a wood fire like this one when the boys decided that they were too, quote, 'big' for hot dogs," using her fingers to make mock air quotes and smiling at her boys.

"So, that's the story of the smörgåsbord and the s'mores. Now I have another story I can't believe I've never shared with the boys, or with you either, Carolina."

And, so, amidst the sounds of the crackling fire, a cardinal looking down on us from a bare oak tree over in our yard, and the four of us sucking the s'mores off our sticks, dear Marge Marshall told us a story that I've thought about often with a smile over the years.

Looking in turn from Ben to Alf and then briefly to me, she began. "Boys, you know your dad and I moved back here, where we both were born, after we attended the College of Charleston and got married the weekend after graduation. But what I've never told you and Car is what came next in those early years back in Travelers Rest.

"It's ultimately the story of your names, Ben and Alf, but it's going to take me a while to get to that, so bear with me, you three. I've honestly never told this story in its entirety to anyone. Only your dad knew all of it.

"Much like you and Alf, Carolina, Ben and Alf's father, Jack, and I became what you'd call a couple when we were sixteen, after being best friends for as long we could remember." As she said this, I couldn't help but look over at Ben, who was staring at his half-eaten marshmallow. And Alf, rather than looking at me, like I'd expected, was also staring at Ben.

When I cast my gaze back to Marge, she smiled at me knowingly before continuing. "The big problem with making the shift from just friends to boyfriend and girlfriend that summer was that your dad's father, despite outward appearances, didn't like me at all. He treated me like the daughter he never had whenever anyone was around, but I later learned that he went to his grave thinking I wasn't good enough for his lone son and sole heir.

"As you know, he would end up outliving his son. But you may not know that, ironically, I ended up being his sole heir. Of course, he got the last laugh, because he died in debt," she said with a nervous chuckle that was meant to lighten the moment but really didn't.

"Well, while his dad was still very much alive, your father and I were married, and he took the one and only job he ever had at the Ford dealership in town. Actually, that's not quite true. As y'all know, he did also sign on for what he called his part-time job with the South Carolina National Guard, and I think that was the week before he started working at the dealership.

"He'd go to what they called weekend drill once a month and then to summer camp for two weeks every year. Even more than he liked wearing his mechanic's overalls with his name on his chest, he loved wearing his different enlisted uniforms. After a couple of years, some colonel convinced him to apply for Officer Candidate School and he was accepted. So, boys, your dad was a second lieutenant infantry officer in the National Guard. I've told you some of that already, right?"

Both Alf and Ben nodded before their mom continued her tale. "Well, that gets me to your names. You know the story behind your name, Alf, which was easy to come up with because I wanted to name our firstborn after my grandfather, Alvar, my mom's father, who I mentioned earlier. Your great-grandfather went by Alf his entire life, so your dad and I decided to keep it simple for you and just name you Alf from the start. Ben, if you'd come first, you'd actually be Alf," she said, smiling at Ben.

"But, for some reason, we had never really talked too much about a second male name once we heard we were having twin boys. I'm not sure why. We just didn't. I guess maybe we were overwhelmed with preparing the house for two babies at once.

"Well, before we knew you two were going to bless our lives, your father had gone to some sort of infantry training down in Georgia, and they required him to stay down there for two weeks. They did let me visit your dad one weekend and spend the night, however. And, as I told you, I've never shared this with anyone." She paused and all of a sudden broke out in a broad grin before saying, "You actually could have been named Benning, Ben!"

At that I looked back and forth between her, Alf, and Ben—and it hit me first. I broke out in a wide smile, slapped my thigh, and practically shouted my question. "You're saying this was Fort Benning, Georgia, and these two were born nine months after that visit, aren't you, Mrs. Marshall? Um, Marge!"

Ben immediately started laughing, saying, "That's totally gross and way too much information, Mom! How do you expect us to eat the rest of these s'mores now?"

I turned to Alf, who had always been the first to get a joke. He finally broke out into a grin. "That's a great story, Mom. And, since I came first, I guess that means two pieces of Sweeee-dish apple cake for me when we're back inside," he said, drawing out the "e" like he always did on Christmas Day, and glancing from Ben to me to his mom with the old smirk I had longed to see again.

Alf gobbled those slices of tasty apple cake, and Ben couldn't resist a second helping as well, but the old Alf didn't last past the four of us sharing dish duty back in the kitchen. He seemed determined to be morose around us. However, I'll always remember that Christmas Day for learning the story of Ben's name.

I typically stayed at the Marshalls' house most of Christmas afternoon, talking about the presents everyone had received and reminiscing over the past year. But Christmas 2000 was quite different, in that it seemed like there were only three people in the room instead of four. Alf was almost a ghost in his own house, and the strain of trying to include him in our conversations finally led me to head back to my house earlier than usual. My excuse was that my dad needed help programming their new bedroom television, which was their Christmas gift to each other. Dad had already set it up that morning without an issue. It was a lie and the first one I can remember telling any of them, actually.

Unable to stop thinking about Alf when I got home, I found

myself researching his name on the internet that evening using my parent's AOL connection. I first looked up "Alvar" and learned that it was originally a German name meaning "elf warrior," which made me smile. My warrior was certainly no elf; both he and Ben had always been of average stature. I also read about a famous Finnish furniture designer named Alvar Aalt, thinking it might be fun to surprise Alf, or even his mom, with at Aalt-designed chair or something, if I could afford it one day.

When I then searched the internet for "Alf," I found that quite a few Scandinavians had the name or went by it as a nickname or shortened name. There was also a Swedish Army major general named Alf Sandqvist, who I told Alf about the next day.

Of course, I couldn't help also reading about the 1966 film *Alfie* and the generally horrid character played by Michael Caine in the film. That led me to the hit Burt Bacharach song, "What's It All About, Alfie." I even listened to Dionne Warwick sing it at the 1967 Grammys, as well as a touching version by Barbra Streisand that was recorded live. I took note of the lyrics near the end, which said, "When you walk, let your heart lead the way." I just hoped my poor Alf's march through The Citadel and beyond wouldn't lead to him losing his way—or my heart.

BEN

———◆———

MY MOTHER'S STORY about Fort Benning and my name seemed to lighten Alf's mood, but it didn't last long. For the first time in our short lives, I seemed to have lost my bond with him. And though the connection that I'd had with Carolina had changed when she and Alf became a couple, I found the shared feelings with and about her fading as well. I think she may have felt all this too, with her leaving our house on Christmas Day earlier than I could remember from years past.

That night, Alf again went upstairs to his room right after a quick dinner of smörgåsbord leftovers. My mom and I remained in the kitchen, drying dishes, and I broached the touchy topic that I felt had been in the air since Thanksgiving.

"Do you think Alf needs some professional help, Mom?"

She paused in the middle of drying a plate, put it back on the counter along with the towel, and said, "I've thought about it a lot, Ben. I keep thinking this is something they should handle at The Citadel. They've probably had many similar issues with other boys over the years."

"Yeah, I'll bet so," I responded. "They've told us at VMI that counseling is always there for us if we're struggling with classes, but that it's also available to Rats, and even upperclassmen, who may be caving in to the inevitable stress outside the classroom."

"Why don't you seem to be having the same problems, Ben? I

just don't know what to do."

"I keep thinking that something specific happened to him down there that hasn't happened to me at VMI. At least not yet. I've asked him about it several times, and he always says no, but he never looks me in the eye when he says it. Can you maybe call someone at The Citadel to see if anyone can help? What about that senior mentor that Alf mentioned, or maybe the ROTC advisor he told us about? My dyke, Brent, would know what to do. Maybe I should ask him."

"No, I don't want your brother to think you're meddling. I feel like the relationship between you two is, for the first time in your lives, strained."

"I know what you mean. He used to tell me—and Carolina—everything."

"Me too. Or at least I thought so."

"He definitely did, Mom. I did as well. You've always made us feel like we could share everything with you and not get in trouble. I do think things had already started changing between Alf and me when Carolina chose him," I continued, putting thoughts into words that I'd not been able to express previously. "This whole Citadel thing goes way beyond Carolina choosing the wrong Marshall boy," I added.

My mother laughed and slapped me lightly with a dish towel. "Well, I'm glad someone can joke about this, Ben. Are you still mad at her?"

"I don't think 'mad' is the right word, Mom. At least not now. It's been years, and I've mostly come to terms with it. But I guess it still hurts. I think what I resent most of all is how it not only changed the relationship between the three of us but also changed the relationship between me and Alf and me and Carolina, separately. Does that make sense?"

Without waiting for a response, I continued my train of thought. "Plus, I don't think any of it can ever be the same again, and it just makes me sad. I hate to admit it to you, but I've felt less resentful about her choice since we've all gone off to college and I've had much bigger fish to fry, so to speak. I'm honestly not sure I could handle having a girlfriend during my Rat year. Even if it was Carolina, who I still love with all of my heart. Just in a different way, I guess, now."

"I know what you mean. I sometimes wonder if that's not part of Alf's struggles. But I really don't think that's it. I think it's all about The Citadel and either something specific that happened down there or just the whole Knob system that has him so rattled."

"I wish there was something we could do, Mom."

"I know, I know. I've mostly decided to give it until your spring breaks to see if he's still in a funk. If he is, I'm just going to have to call The Citadel."

"That sounds like a good plan, Mom. I feel so helpless."

"Me too, Ben. He'll get through this. And so will you."

We then headed to the living room and spent yet another evening reading in front of the little gas fireplace. I distinctly remember reading *A Farewell to Arms* to get ahead for my second-semester English class, and I think she was reading Patricia Cornwell's *Southern Cross*, or maybe one of her other thrillers. I've always had a strange knack for remembering where I was when I read books and, usually, what my mother was reading if we were together. Later, that would be true for another person I love more than words can express.

PART III

ALF

THERE'S LITTLE TO tell of my second semester in 2001, except that it was much like the previous one, with the continued physical, mental, and military challenges of simply being a lowly Citadel Knob. Well, at least until Recognition Day in March. Before that day, I kept my eyes and mind straight ahead. My classes provided a welcome distraction from both barracks life and my time as a Knob elsewhere on campus.

I enjoyed the structure of military life and still envisioned a career in the Marine Corps long past the four-plus years required by my scholarship. Carolina had told me several times that she would support me and my career choice one-hundred-percent, but I knew my behavior since August had given her pause. During the long nights lying in my bed back in barracks, I told myself that I would start being more open with her—and my brother and mother—when I went home for our short Easter furlough in April.

The bad times were many at The Citadel that first year, and we had lost about sixty classmates during our first semester and over Christmas furlough, but fewer Knobs were leaving as Recognition Day and the tough first year's end approached.

They say that your three best days at The Citadel are Recognition Day, when you're no longer a Knob, the day you get your class ring the fall of senior year, and graduation day. At the time, Recognition Day's importance seemed to pale in comparison to getting our rings and graduating, but I will say that losing the physical and mental stresses of being a Knob that spring day in 2001 helped quell my general moodiness and seriousness.

On Recognition Day, a cloudy Friday, we were awakened early to go for yet another run before returning to barracks for our last push-ups as Knobs. Then, in unison, my company and the others recited the cadet prayer:

> Almighty God, the source of light and strength, we implore Thy blessing on this our beloved institution, that it may continue true to its high purposes.
>
> Guide and strengthen those upon whom rests the authority of government; enlighten with wisdom those who teach and those who learn; and grant to all of us that through sound learning and firm leadership, we may prove ourselves worthy citizens of our country, devoted to truth, given to unselfish service, loyal to every obligation of life and above all to Thee.
>
> Preserve us faithful to the ideals of The Citadel, sincere in fellowship, unswerving in duty, finding joy in purity, and confidence through a steadfast faith.
>
> Grant to each one of us, in his (her) own life, a humble heart, a steadfast purpose, and a joyful hope, with a readiness to endure hardship and suffer if need be, that truth may prevail among us and that Thy will may be done on earth.
>
> Through Jesus Christ, Our Lord. Amen.

Of course, I'd memorized the prayer, which was composed for The Citadel's centennial back in 1942 by Bishop Albert S. Thomas, Class of 1892. I knew that several of my classmates and upperclassmen chose not to recite the last line of the cadet prayer, based on their religious beliefs, but noticed that many of those who did recite every word seemed to raise their voices for the last line to compensate for those who didn't.

After the prayer, the announcement came over the loudspeaker, which had become such a part of the narrative of my Knob year. The deep voice said, "The Fourth Class system is no longer in effect." With that, a cheer rose throughout barracks, and I hugged lots of my company's classmates, as well as shaking hands with several upperclassmen—even those who had given me a hard time the last few months. However, I did not shake the hand of one particular senior. Not that it was proffered.

Following a barbeque lunch in barracks that remains one of the best meals I'd have on campus, we marched downtown to Marion Square, the site of the original Citadel, which is now a popular Embassy Suites where my mom and Carolina occasionally stayed during my cadetship and would for graduation. Once in Marion Square, we said the Cadet Oath in unison:

> I, Alf Marshall, hereby engage to serve as a cadet in The Citadel, the Military College of South Carolina, until graduation or until I shall be discharged by proper authority; and I promise to support loyally the constituted authorities thereof as long as I remain a member of the corps of cadets.
>
> I will remain loyal to the ideals, values, and goals of the citadel. I further promise that I will never bring discredit on the citadel or the South Carolina Corps of Cadets. I take this obligation freely and without any mental reservation or purpose of evasion.

BEN

——◆——

THEY HAD A saying at VMI about Rats that you'd start the Ratline with leaves on the trees, and that they'd drop come fall, and you'd still be in the Ratline. Come winter, you'd wake up in the dark and fall asleep in the dark—and you'd still be in the Ratline. Spring would come, the leaves would return. And you'd still be in the Ratline.

I was beginning to think this was really true when we got to mid-February and we were still Rats. But we finally experienced what's long been called "Breakout." Ironically, I didn't find it as hard as I thought it might be. I was a very different person—physically and mentally—than the one who reported to VMI back in August. Of course, the sweat parties and other physical and mental pressures intensified leading up to Breakout, and so did the jokes from Thirds that we wouldn't get out of the Ratline until May. If ever.

I'd heard this always happened and didn't take it too seriously, but I still couldn't wait for Breakout to mark my first truly important accomplishment at VMI—besides not leaving, I guess. And Breakout finally happened for us in late February.

After seemingly endless mornings and nights of runs and sweat parties, Breakout for the Class of 2004 began in earnest on a brisk and cloudy Saturday afternoon. We had gone for a fourteen-mile march, followed by a sweat party given by the First Class that night.

The next day, we had several other sweat parties, and they also took us out on a difficult run of several miles with our rifles. My shoulders still ache at the memory, and Virginia told me hers do as well whenever she remembers that particular outing on the Chessie Trail.

It was by far the most intense few days of workouts our burgeoning class would face. They awoke us a bit before five on Wednesday for another long run. Then, after a shortened class schedule and a quick change into fatigues, we were taken into Jackson Memorial Hall for a speech about the fabled VMI family by the First Class president.

We then ran over to New Barracks for whatever would come next.

What came next was Breakout. It started with a short but intense sweat party in New Barracks, with my dripping sweat turning immediately chilly in the February air. Then the upperclassmen leading Breakout sent about a hundred of us at a time down to the rifle range, where I was in the screaming first group of Rats charging up the hill as Seconds pushed us back down. The Seconds finally allowed us to pass. Then we had to make our way through a muddy pit filled with Thirds, who made our trip through the muck as messy and slow as possible.

Once our three groups had passed through these two trials, we ran back up to the Parade Ground for a final short workout before being sent into Old Barracks. There, the Class of 2004 officially came into existence with our first "old yell," which I assume has been yelled by classes at VMI for decades but have never checked:

> Rah Virginia Mil
> Rah Rah Rah
> Rah Rah, VMI, '04, '04, '04.

It bounced off the walls of Old Barracks like old yells had for decades. We then gave old yells for our dykes in the Class of '01 and even somewhat begrudgingly for the classes of '02 and '03.

That night we shared a steak dinner with our dykes down in the mess hall. Mine was cooked perfectly medium rare, if I recall. Virginia still smiles at the memory of that meal and swears her steak was overcooked.

Everyone in our newly formed class thought there would be a letdown after Breakout, but it certainly didn't happen that first spring. But though we still had much less freedom than they had at Washington & Lee next door, and almost every other college in the country, it felt like we were at a very different college after we became the Class of 2004.

It was hard to pinpoint just one thing that made the difference, and trying to explain it to an outsider remains futile. But regaining small human pleasures and privileges made all the difference that damp spring in Lexington. The lack of large, time-consuming requirements like walking the Ratline, physical and mental Rat challenges, and eating square meals, as well as seemingly small things like being allowed to walk across the Parade Ground instead of around it, all made the endless only-at-VMI things easier to bear.

A wet March, when everything on post remained gray, including our uniforms, finally turned to April. We returned to the white uniforms we'd worn in late summer and into fall, which brought back memories of our first week in green fatigues and the bleak period at the beginning of the Ratline, when no end seemed in sight.

Since they'd never need their gray wool uniform pants again, the Firsts, including my dyke, Brent Dunaway, burned them in the Old Barracks courtyard. As I watched from the fourth stoop, I couldn't help but think about what it would be like in three years to be down in the courtyard, burning my own woolies. I did that a lot at VMI, witnessing decades-old rituals of those ahead of me and dreaming about the day I would follow in their footsteps.

CAROLINA

———o———

IN JANUARY, I returned to Chapel Hill with a heavy heart for Alf, still very much missing the life we'd once led. However, my new life at UNC marched forward, with my classes, Tri Sig, and small tasks at *The Daily Tar Heel* keeping me busy and generally content from morning to night. It was only late at night under my grandmother's handmade quilt that I thought about the Upcountry and, inevitably, Alf and The Citadel. And dear Ben and Marge.

Since he'd accepted his Marine Corps scholarship to The Citadel, I'd consistently and frequently told Alf that I'd be by his side wherever his life led him and us, with or without the Marine Corps. I couldn't help but wonder on those cold Chapel Hill nights in my dorm room if Alf was ever going to come out of what I began to believe was some sort of depression.

I kept thinking that once the pressures of his time as a Knob ended, it would be better. I think that's what we all hoped.

Back at Carolina after Easter, I was asked to become a staff writer for the paper, specializing in sorority news. Later, my role expanded, and it was a great way to get to know other girls on campus over the next three-plus years.

I hadn't wanted to jinx it, but once I got a regular gig, I decided to buy everything in the school's bookstore that was Charles Kuralt-related. There was a lot. If I remember correctly, my booty over a three-week period in late April included paperback versions of *On the Road with Charles Kuralt,* which remains my favorite, *Charles Kuralt's America,* and *Charles Kuralt: A Life on the Road.* Those books, and later ones like Ralph Grizzle's *Remembering Charles Kuralt,* had a major influence on my decision to become a journalist. I also loved buying used cassettes and CDs that Kuralt had produced, his famous baritone voice taking me to places across the country that I someday hoped to explore as well.

When I wasn't studying for classes, writing for the paper, or volunteering for something with Tri Sig, I devoured these books and everything else I could find on Kuralt, who had become my idol and absentee mentor.

My freshman year soon came to an end. Like many, including Ben and Alf, it was a year that shaped the rest of my life in ways we never could have expected.

ALF

———■———

I HONESTLY CAN'T say I was glad that my Knob year was coming to an end come mid-May. My time at home was somehow harder than life on campus in Charleston. Of course, I could never explain this to the most important people in my life.

Graduation day for the upperclassmen on the twelfth provided the first college commencement ceremony I'd attended, and though I already knew it in many ways, I quickly learned that graduating from The Citadel was unlike graduating from any college in America. I know grads of service academies, as well as VMI, would disagree, but there's something truly unique about graduation day at The Citadel, where certain traditions, like the "Last Graduate," provide only-at-The Citadel moments.

Though I longed for that day, I also knew I had much to learn from my fellow cadets and the military staff across campus. I knew I would be ready to be a Marine Corps officer by the time I walked across the stage at McAlister Field House. And I was.

What I remember most about graduation for The Citadel's class of 2001 was the commencement speaker. In a twist of pre-9/11 fate, Pat Conroy, Class of 1967, was welcomed back to The Citadel with partially open arms to provide what remains for me and others one of the best college commencement speeches ever.

Given what was to happen later that year, it seemed fitting that Conroy, who knew a few things about words, life, and death, would give the commencement speech for the Class of 2001. I looked it up later, and here's what he said on that sunny May day:

> General Grinalds; the Board of Visitors; Lt. Col Thomas Nugent Courvoisie, the Boo, in my first book; Greg and Mary Wilson Smith, The Citadel family who did more than anyone else to bring me back to my Citadel family; Skip Wharton; Rogers Harrell, member of the class of '01, lost his father last year, and his father will not be able to hand him his diploma, but members of the class of '71 have rallied here because of the love of that father.
>
> Class of 2001, listen up, I don't have much time. They don't give you that much time for graduation speeches. Because of various aspects of my character and fates, I did not get to address the Corps of Cadets in the last century. There were many years when I thought that Saddam Hussein or Jane Fonda had a better chance of addressing this class than I did.
>
> In 1979, the year most of y'all were born, I was finishing up *The Lords of Discipline*, and I tried to think of a line or words that would sum up better than anything how I felt and how other people feel about this college. I wanted it to be something ringing and affirmative, something true, something to be true for every person who has ever gone through the long gray line. I came up with this line: "I wear the ring."
>
> I think it is the best line I have ever written and the best English sentence I am capable of writing. I love that phrase. I love that sentence. Thirty-four years ago, I sat in this field house—my mother and father, my six brothers and sisters, sitting in the audience as your parents are sitting now.
>
> My parents—it was their proudest day. My mother wept when I came off the stage that day. She wept so hard, and I said, "Mom, what's wrong?" And she said, "Son, you are the first person in my family who has ever graduated from college,

and you did it at The Citadel." And she said, "The best college in America."

Let me tell you something about that mother. Here's my mother's socioeconomic status exactly. Everything you need to know about my family . . . from her mother's family name. My grandfather, Jasper Catholic Peak; his brother, Cicero. Then there's Vashtye, Taleatha, Clyde, Pluma.

And my favorite—I was cleaning up a grave with my grandmother, Stanny, and I came across this name, "Jerry Mire Peak"—okay, that's Jerry Mire—M-I-R-E Peak. And I said, "Stanny, who is he named after?" And she said, "He is named after the prophet Jerrymire."

My father was a different case. My father, six-foot-three, 230-pound Marine Corps fighter pilot, knuckles dragging along the ground when he walked. When he was dying, I interviewed Dad. I said, "Dad, tell me about what it was like in the war."

He told me about coming off the aircraft carrier *Sicily* in Korea. His was the first squadron that got there, and they said, "Keep the Koreans north of the Naktong River." So, he dove down—the first plane the North Koreans had seen—he dove down toward the enemy. I said, "How did you do, Dad?"

He said, "I did pretty good, son." He said, "I had a good sign—they were running. It's good when you see the enemy running. There was another good sign, son."

"What's that, Dad?"

"They were on fire."

That was the man who dandled me on his knee when I was a young boy—the Great Santini. I once introduced my father when I was giving a talk like this, and I said, "My father decided to go in the Marine Corps when he found out that his IQ was the temperature of this room."

My father got up right behind me. He stared down at the

audience and he said, "My God, it's hot in here . . . it must be at least 165 degrees."

These were the people who raised me, the people who inspired me. They sent me to this college. They did not ask me where I wanted to go. Both of them wanted me to go here.

My father applied to this college. I did not. I never saw an application. Never signed an application, but ended up here in 1963 for Hell Week. I remember Hell Week. I don't know how you did it, kids, but they did it good back then, I want to tell you.

And after Hell Night, I remember going there—it was a vivid experience—an upperclassman came and said, "Mr. Conroy, you look tired, exhausted. Why don't you come to my room and just hang out for a while?"

The next thing I knew I was hanging from the pipes in his room. And I realized that I had come to a place that has etched itself on me, etched itself on my character. I have written more about my college than any writer in American history. My book will be coming out next year—it will be the third book I have written about this college. And I write about it because I cannot keep away from it . . . the experience, it's so fresh and fiery on my imagination.

And, because it's a great relationship, I wanted to tell you something seriously. I wanted to tell my Citadel family how I got involved in the great war of bringing women to this college. After I wrote *The Lords of Discipline* in 1980 and the reaction of this school, kids, Conroy ain't stupid. This is a tough place.

And I said, "Okay, I have gotten through that," and I was retiring from the field for the rest of my life. I was speaking in colleges in the Northeast. I spoke at Harvard, the Rhode Island School of Design. And then I was looking down at the next college I was supposed to speak at, and to my amazement, it was the Coast Guard Academy.

Ladies and Gentlemen, the class of 2001, you probably think I speak at military colleges a lot, but after *The Lords of Discipline*, the invitations—I got one invitation from VMI. The man who invited me was fired the next day.

So, I called my wife, and I said, "There's the Coast Guard Academy. I cannot possibly speak there."

She said, "Yeah, they pay you money."

So, I went to the Coast Guard Academy and was met by the guy who invited me, and he said, "Mr. Conroy, I had no idea inviting you would be such a stir." He said, "The commandant told me if you said anything that irritated him that he would fire me even though I had tenure."

So, I said, "What do you think I'm going to do, call for the dissolution of the American armed forces?" I said. "This will be great."

The commandant flew up from Washington. He sat there stern faced. I like the way generals can be stern. So, he was sitting there stern faced, and I talked to the group, but first of all, I had gone to talk to the freshmen. I talked to these freshmen, and I looked out there, and 25 percent of them were women. I said, "What are you girls doing here? Are you crazy? Are you nuts?"

And one of them there, the woman who was leading me around, said, "Sir, they let women in the academies in 1974."

And I said to these freshmen girls, "Is it as horrible for y'all as it was for me when I was a freshman?"

A couple of them go—you can't say anything naturally—but a couple of these young women went . . .

And, here, Conroy simply nodded before continuing.

I talked to the Coast Guard Academy that night. I had a

ball. I want to tell y'all something—I can talk to a corps of cadets. I talked to them about what happened to me at The Citadel. We roared with laughter. Military colleges—we have common experiences; we share common things. When they took me to the plane the next day, the four women—I asked them—I said, "What are you going to do when you get out of here?"

One of the women said, "Fly an attack helicopter, sir."

"No kidding. What are you going to do?"

"Drive a ship, sir."

So, they helped me off then, these four accursed Coast Guard Academy women. And right before I got on the plane, one said, "How'd you like the Coast Guard Academy?"

"I loved it."

Then one of them said, "How'd you like us, sir? How'd you like the women at the Coast Guard Academy?"

I said, "I loved y'all. What's not to like? You're sharp cadets—funny, smart."

One of them then said, the trap then being set, "Mr. Conroy, when a woman applies at The Citadel, will you help her out? Will you support her? She's not going to have much."

I said, "Listen, gals, you don't know The Citadel. That is *never* going to happen in my lifetime. It's not even a chance, and you just don't know The Citadel."

And one of the women said, "Mr. Conroy, you don't know women."

In the early-nineties I received a letter from one of those accursed Coast Guard women. "Mr. Conroy, the first woman has applied to The Citadel. We remember your talk. Your talk is famous at the Coast Guard Academy. We especially remember your talking about your time on the honor courts, how much that meant to you. How much that changed you. How much that set your character. And we know because you promised to support the first woman that we can count on you because, like you, we have an honor system we believe in. Her name is Shannon Faulkner. And we know you'll do your duty."

I tore that letter up. I said, "These women are going to get me killed." But I'm a Citadel man, and they mentioned the honor code. And there's a lot wrong with me, class of 2001, except this—I know what the meaning of "is" is.

While writing this latest book *My Losing Season*, I interviewed all the basketball players, the boys I loved from this gymnasium . . . I adored them. They did not know it. I went back to meet all of them, but one meeting changed my life. I went back to see Al Kroboth, center, class of 1969, a POW, a Marine in Vietnam. I sat him down and I said, "Al, you got to tell me about being a POW. You got to tell me everything, but I'm a novelist—you got to let me know how it feels."

"Can I have my wife, Patty, be with me?"

"Sure."

An interview I thought would take an hour took seven. And I said, "Al, history is going to come between us." And history is going come all over this, class of 2001. And I said, "Al, I was a draft dodger. I was a Vietnam protester during the war . . . you need to know this before we talk."

He said, "Conroy, you did what you did. I did what I did. I'm fine."

Then he proceeds to tell me about the most harrowing Vietnam experience I've ever heard of where he is shot down. He wakes up with an AK-47 pointed at his face. He has a broken back, a shattered scapula. They tell him to get up and Al Kroboth, who is in South Vietnam, in the jungle walks barefoot at night for three months through the Vietnam jungle in the most horrible, tortured thing I have ever heard about in my life.

I said, "Al, how did you make it? How'd you do the pain, the leeches, the boils, the bites—everything?" I said, "How'd you make it?"

Al Kroboth looks at me and says, "The plebe system. I made it because of the plebe system. I made it because I'm a Citadel man."

He gets along. He's in terrible, terrible confinement in North Vietnam. Then I said, "Tell me when you got out, Al. Tell me how it felt."

He talked about the plane landing. Al's a Marine, like the general. And Al is standing there. "I didn't feel anything, Conroy. And then the plane, I saw it go down to the end of the field, and I saw it turn, and I saw the American flag." And, as Al Kroboth said he saw the American flag, he wept. His wife wept. Then I wept.

He said then the plane takes off and all of the POWs are in this plane, and he says he's not feeling anything. And then the pilot comes on and says, "Feet wet. Feet wet. We have left North Vietnamese territory."

And Al Kroboth weeps again, and his wife weeps.

The North Vietnamese told them that Americans hated the war. They were hated. That they were considered war criminals. So, when Al landed, and all of the other POWs in the Philippines, they got a hero's welcome from 10,000 people . . . he was shocked when he walked through that crowd, through a red carpet and a little girl sitting on her father's shoulders handed him a piece of paper. He didn't look at it until he got on the bus. And in this childish scrawl, this girl had written, "Greater love than this, no man hath."

And Al Kroboth broke again. His wife broke. I broke.

Then Al, on the tenth floor being debriefed, he gets a call that there's a Citadel man waiting for him down in the lobby, so he takes an officer down there, and he goes down to the lobby, and Johnny Vaughan, who had been a cheerleader on my basketball team—Johnny used to jump up and down for me and Al—Johnny Vaughan is waiting for Al Kroboth.

And he gets down there, and they embrace, and then Johnny says, "Al, I heard you lost your Citadel ring."

And Al said, "The Vietcong stole it."

And then, what to me is one of the great moments in Citadel history—Johnny Vaughan took off his Citadel ring and said, "I'm not letting you go back to America without wearing a Citadel ring."

He said, "No, Johnny, I can't do it. I've lost too much weight. I'll lose it."

He said, "No, no. Listen to me, I'm not letting you go back to America without wearing a Citadel ring."

And he took Al's hand and he put his ring on Al Kroboth's hand.

Class of 2001, I brought an audiovisual aid for you today. I wanted to bring the type of alumni you are capable of turning yourselves into. I would like Al Kroboth and Johnny Vaughan to stand up and meet the class of 2001. Where are you guys?

At this, I remember Kroboth and Vaughan stood, and then all of us rose to our feet as one and gave them a standing ovation before Conroy continued minutes later.

In closing, class of 2001, I cannot thank y'all enough for doing this for me. I did not exactly pencil this speech into my schedule of coming attractions, and you do me the highest honor by bringing me fully into my Citadel family. And I was trying to think of something I can do because a graduation speaker needs to speak of time—time passing. Usually, I tell graduation classes I want them to think of me on their fortieth birthday, but I got something else I want to do for y'all because I'm so moved at what you've done for me. I would like to invite each one of you in the class of 2001 to my funeral, and I mean that. I will not be having a good day that day . . . but I have told my wife and my heirs that I wanted the class of 2001 to have an honored place whenever my funeral takes place.

And I hope as many of you will come as you possibly can because I want you to know how swift time is, and there is nothing as swift—and you know this—from the day you walked into Lesesne Gate until this day—a heartbeat, an eye blink. This is the way life is. It is the only great surprise in life.

So, I'm going to tell you how to get to my funeral. You walk up . . . You find the usher waiting outside, and here's your ticket . . . You put up your Citadel ring. Let them check for the 2001, and each one of you, I want you to say this before you enter the church at which I'm going to be buried. You tell them, "I wear the ring."

Thank you so much.

I never saw Pat Conroy again, but if I had, I would have told him that his speech gave me more determination than ever to wear the ring proudly, and to serve my country at peace or during war. And if I had it to do again, I would have found Mr. Kroboth and Mr. Vaughan that day, or later in life, to tell them as well. I would think of all three men at times when I called upon my experience as a Knob to be The Citadel man they described.

About two weeks before graduation, my ROTC advisor asked me to stay back in Charleston for a few days to work on a project for him, where I'd actually get paid by the Marine Corps. I'll have to admit that I welcomed a delay of my return to TR for the summer.

BEN

——————◆——————

IN MID-MAY, ON the seventeenth, I attended the first of four VMI graduation ceremonies as a cadet. It was great to see my dyke, Brent, walk across the Cameron Hall stage, and relatively easy to picture myself doing it three years later. I also remember Virginia's dyke, Laura, crossing the stage. She was one of just a dozen or so groundbreaking females to graduate from VMI in May, making them the first female cadets to survive four years at the Institute. While a few of the two-dozen-plus females who started at VMI in 1997 came to school as upperclassmen and graduated early, about half of the original female Rats had dropped out for varying reasons. I knew Virginia was very proud of Laura and would continue to emulate her in many ways.

The commencement speaker that day was the late Senator John McCain, who died in 2018 after a courageous battle with brain cancer. I remember he spoke that May day of his five long years as a prisoner of war in Vietnam, and he advised all of us to choose our careers—and causes, if I remember correctly—carefully.

That was certainly true for all military school graduates anytime, but especially with what was to come later that year, when many careers and causes would revolve around the war on terrorism.

I remembered Senator McCain's words in 2015, when he was attacked by a presidential candidate who became the nation's commander in chief, saying McCain wasn't a war hero. That comment came from a man who, by all accounts, successfully dodged the draft.

When McCain died in 2018, I dug up his speech and found this nugget: "I discovered that nothing is more liberating than to fight for a cause larger than yourself—something that encompasses you, but is not defined by your existence alone." Those were the words of a true patriot and hero, in war and peace.

VMI's graduation didn't coincide with UNC's, and the now-graduated First, Matt, who'd given me a ride back home every time that first year seemed disappointed that we weren't picking Carolina up again. A half hour or so into the drive, as we passed the exit for Hollins, he said, "I think Carolina liked me, don't you, Rat?"

"Hey now, Matt, I'm a Third now. Not that it means very much at VMI."

"I hear ya. But you'll find that with each year at VMI, the little stuff means a lot. I have to say I found Second Class year and this year a walk in the park compared to my first two years. I think most of my classmates would agree. But don't you think that girl liked me?"

I laughed, saying, "She only has eyes for one guy in uniform and, incredibly, he's my twin brother, who is finishing up his first year at The Citadel. Remember, we talked about his struggles down in Charleston the last time Carolina and I rode with you?"

"Oh yeah. I remember now. You two are certainly gluttons for punishment. But, heck, even I'd go to The Citadel for a day if that girl'd take a roll in the hay with me."

I knew it was just gutter-mouth, boy-man talk, but I couldn't resist quickly responding in a bit too loud of a voice, "Carolina's like a sister to me, Matt, and I'd appreciate it if you didn't speak of her that way, even if you're joking."

"Hey now, you know I'm just foolin around. I don't mess with other men's women. Especially boyfriends who know how to fire an M-16. Besides, you know I'm happily engaged, right?"

"Yeah, I remember. I did notice you didn't seem to mention that to Carolina during any of our rides this year."

"Just because you've ordered doesn't mean you can't still look at the menu," he said, looking over at me with a smile that bordered on a leer.

"Good point, I guess. When are you getting married, anyway?"

"Next Saturday, actually," he replied as we drove into Travelers Rest, heading toward my house. "We're going back to VMI on Friday afternoon, and the chaplain is going to marry us in Jackson Chapel. Mary Jo will then have three rings. A miniature of my ring, the engagement ring, and her wedding band, which reminds me that I need to pick it up tomorrow down on Haywood at Hale's."

"The only ring I care about is the one I'll be getting at VMI—in about eighteen months, I guess."

"It'll get here before you know it, as long as you continue to toe the line in your classes, barracks, and with the Honor Court, like you say you're doing." He turned to me for affirmation.

"I will," I replied firmly, locking eyes with him just as he pulled up to our house.

Like I had for years, I went around back to enter through the kitchen, and like every other time I'd returned to TR, Mom was there waiting for me. "Welcome home, Ben." She smiled, walking the short ten feet from the stove to the door to hug me.

"Thanks, Mom," I said, releasing her from our embrace and looking toward the counter. "What's cookin'?"

"Oh, you know, Ben," she said, still smiling. "It's always chocolate chip cookies for you two when you return to the nest. Plus, I have a meatloaf in the oven."

"Where's Alf?" I asked.

"Oh, he ended up staying down at The Citadel to work on some project for his Navy ROTC advisor. He says he's coming home tomorrow or the next day."

"That's the first I've heard of that. I thought he'd be anxious to get out of Charleston. I sure was ready to head home. Carolina's home though, right?"

"Yep, she is. She was over here waiting for you but had to head back home to help her mom with something. Why don't you go call or go over there to see if she wants to join us for meatloaf tonight?"

A few hours later, Carolina did come over for dinner, and looking back, I hate to admit how much I enjoyed that evening in our home without Alf. There was simply less tension in the air and a lot more words and thoughts than if Alf had been with us. We never spoke of his issues and silences, and it felt good to have a happy time in our house.

Both Carolina and my mom also seemed more at ease, as if Alf's absence had returned us to a simpler time. At least, it was seemingly simpler before The Citadel, and before Carolina made her choice.

Carolina stayed to eat a single chocolate chip cookie for dessert, with my mother having two and saying through a mouthful that she could see how Carolina was avoiding the dreaded "freshman fifteen." Carolina laughed and said through her own crumb-filled mouth that the cafeteria food at UNC was forcing her on a diet not of her choosing. I'd been eating VMI mess hall food for most of the last eight months, as well as working it all off with runs and push-ups, so I had three more cookies without any qualms.

Though our conversation seemed easier, Alf's issues still hung in the air with almost every sentence we shared that night. Though never broached, it still seemed to taint everything spoken—and unsaid.

CAROLINA

THAT FIRST NIGHT back from Chapel Hill for summer break was a breath of fresh air compared to other times back home since August. I hated how much I liked that there was no tension in the air when I went over to the Marshalls' house for meatloaf that first night back.

The three of us mostly talked of past summers and our favorite things about them. When Marge asked me what I remembered most, I gave it some thought before saying, "I loved playing in your backyard, from that little swing set to playing Army. Of course, I will always treasure the trips to Edisto, and especially when Ben and Alf were there. And you too, Mrs. Marshall, when you came down for our birthdays and other celebrations. I loved having you there."

"What I don't love is when you keep calling me Mrs. Marshall, Carolina. Please call me Marge."

"Oops. I forgot again . . . Marge. Let's see, what else do I remember? I enjoyed all of the ice cream down at Pickwick's pharmacy, of course. Still do. And walking around Furman's lake. Oh, and wearing Chanel No. 5 for the first time. What about you, Ben?"

"I'm glad you went first, Carolina. You thought of lots I'd include as well, except for the Chanel No. 5, of course. But you also got me thinkin' about some other stuff, like hiking Paris Mountain trails or fishing up on the Saluda. And I'll never forget eating blue crabs on your deck down on Edisto. How 'bout you, Mom?"

"I do love crabs, y'all. Why don't we get a bushel this summer from Joe Joe's and eat 'em out on the back deck? It won't be quite the same as fresh ones from Edisto, but I'd still love it.

"Let's see. What else? How 'bout our trips to downtown Greenville when it started its comeback. I'll always remember treating you three to a belated sixteenth birthday dinner at that restaurant that had just opened. What's the name of it? Soby's, right? I think it had been a shoe store or something."

"Oh, yeah, I remember that dinner!" I said. "We sat at a window overlooking Main Street, which was still kinda rough. Let's get back down there this summer. I hear it's really changing quickly."

I looked over at Marge as I said this, and she had a far-off, thoughtful look in her eyes that seemed to stretch back over the years. We fell silent. I knew she and Ben were both thinking back to a simpler time, before our sixteenth birthdays. When I'd made my choice.

ALF

———————■———————

I OSTENSIBLY STAYED back in Charleston to spend a final afternoon and evening with my senior mentor, Dave Daley, and his family, and then to work on a one- or two-day project in the Naval ROTC Department. Dave was reporting to Fort Benning the next day for the Infantry Officer Basic Course, which everyone called OBC.

I'd jumped at the chance to delay my inevitable return home for the summer. I'm sure that Carolina, my mom, and Ben had figured that out in their own ways.

I'm sure many would find it strange that someone attending a tough military college wouldn't want to get back home for summer break as soon as possible. But that just wasn't me. At least not yet. I kept hoping I could be more like other cadets at The Citadel, or like Ben, but I seemed to carry the weight of my cadetship with me day and night, wherever I was. Somehow, that weight seemed lighter when I was on campus.

After graduation, Dave invited me to dinner with his parents, and I enjoyed the leisurely walk downtown, reaching Hank's Seafood as they were approaching in the opposite direction from the Doubletree, where Dave's parents were staying. Without thinking, I opened the door for Dave's pretty mother. She looked back over her shoulder as she walked in, saying, "I just love the South. And Southern gentlemen."

Dave followed Mrs. Daley, and then Mr. Daley was next. He

looked back to me and said with a smile, "Just keep opening those doors, son, and you'll go far in this world."

I honestly don't remember much of that dinner, except for the tasty seafood platter that Mr. Daley had practically ordered us to order, with me blurting through buttered and spiced fingers, "This restaurant and that shrimp will become reason enough to come back to The Citadel this August. And for two more Augusts after that." I would do just that several times in the coming years, though it wasn't always with the people I would have predicted that May evening.

One other thing about that night that I remember is that, for reasons I'm unsure of, I told the Daleys the story of how Ben got his name. With Dave heading to Fort Benning the next day, all three of them seemed to appreciate the tale, and I envisioned them sharing it with others, just as I had done with the three of them that night.

CAROLINA

———•———○———•———

I WAS FRUSTRATED the following week when Alf returned home, acting just as stoic as ever about anything having to do with The Citadel, even when it was just an offhand question about his life there. He did seem to perk up when we talked about our former lives back in Travelers Rest, so that evening when we were alone in my living room, I asked him, "What are some of your favorite memories about growing up here, Alf?"

After staring into the small springtime fire that my father had built after dinner, Alf said, "Your backyard. This room. The beach. Blue crabs. And the Pickwick's ice cream, of course."

"Good stuff, huh, Alf? Your mom, Ben, and I talked about this when Ben got home from VMI, and at least one of us mentioned every one of those. Doesn't that just make you want some blue crabs this summer? Or how 'bout some ice cream at the Pickwick right now?"

In the past, Alf would have been the first one off the sofa and out the door, which he'd leave open for me or whoever else was following in his wake. But that night he just sat there, before I said, "Come on, Alf, you never turn down a scoop. Or three!"

I got up, grabbed Alf's hand, and dramatically pulled him off the couch, and yelled to my parents in the kitchen that we were headed out to the Pickwick, and that we were borrowing the Volvo. I also yelled to them that we would bring them back their favorite flavors.

I didn't have to ask what they were—butter pecan for Mom and mint moose tracks for Dad.

Alf had let me pull him off the couch somewhat begrudgingly, and I then led him out the door like a horse instead of trying to catch up with him like on our many past outings to the Pickwick and practically anywhere else. Alf was always ready to march on to the next thing, until he marched off to The Citadel.

Once there, we ordered two scoops of chocolate chip cookie dough and said we only needed one spoon. Once we started dating, we always sat at the old soda fountain, feeding each other spoonfuls of ice cream. While one ate, the other would talk about the future. Our future.

Back before I'd chosen Alf over Ben, it was the three of us sharing three different flavors and talking nonstop. However, on this night we sat at our little stools and ate in silence with that single spoon. We then got my parents their ice cream to go before heading home. In silence.

I had really hoped that the longer summer break would allow Alf to take a deep breath and step away from his life at The Citadel, but it just wasn't meant to be. There were hints of my former Alf when we were alone, but whenever we were with Ben or Marge, he returned to whatever place he'd gone the past year.

Once, in early June, when we were sitting on my front porch, Alf's stoicism cracked slightly open, unprovoked. After a long silence when we were simply holding hands, he said, "I'm sorry I've been so quiet whenever we're together, Car. I just can't seem to get outside of my own head with what's happening in Charleston."

This was the first time he'd brought up The Citadel since he got home, and I didn't say anything in response. He continued, "I promise you that I know it's a problem and I'm really working to solve it, but just know this has nothing to do with you, Ben, or my mom. It's between me and The Citadel, and I want to leave it at that." I just squeezed his hand in response and the subject was dropped. Again.

Alf did have a four-week ROTC commitment where he served

onboard the USS *Pensacola*. I never asked him anything about it, and he didn't volunteer a single word about his experience on the ship.

When he returned to TR in mid-July, he told me, "I know I'm still being too quiet with you and everyone else. I'm sorry."

This time, I said, "Just what is it that's happening—or happened—at The Citadel that's changed you so much, Alf?"

At this, he let go of my hand and used it to rub his still-short hair. Staring at the house across from us but grabbing my hand again, he said, "I'm afraid I just can't tell you, Car. It was something that happened at the beginning of the year. But it wouldn't do any good telling you what it was. Only harm. Does that even make sense?"

"I think so," I said, squeezing his hand and using my free one to gently turn him to face me, saying, "But what doesn't make sense to any of us is how you can't leave it back in Charleston like Ben seems to with VMI."

He abruptly let go of my hand but kept my gaze in his, snarling, "I wish all of you would stop trying to compare how Ben and I are handling relatively similar situations differently, Car. Despite what everyone seems to think, we're not clones, and neither are our chosen schools!"

"I know, I know, Alf. Of all people, you should know that I know this. I chose you, didn't I? And one of the reasons was the special way you seemed to treat everything—and everyone—in life. Like it was all a big adventure or something and you were going to take everyone along for the ride. With me by your side. Somehow, that adventurous spirit seems to have left you. What happened, Alf?"

"Damn it, Carolina. I can't tell you!" he said more forcefully, roughly grabbing my hand again and squeezing it a bit too hard. "Let's drop it."

"What does that mean, Alf?" I asked, with the continued frustration surely showing in my tone and eyes.

"Okay. I'll try to put this into words you and others can understand. It means that a specific thing—and everything—that has happened to me down in Charleston is changing me into a very different person.

"From that first night in barracks, I've learned that other people have the ability to do you harm on many levels. And it's not just at The Citadel. The upperclassmen who are going on active duty, as well as several ROTC officers, have been telling me about all of our enemies near and far. Knowing that has transformed the way I look at people, and I'm afraid that even includes you, Ben, and Mom. I truly fear for you three. I'm only ten months into my commitment to the Marine Corps, and I've already changed into someone that wants to protect all of you from harm. And I mean harm around the corner and around the world. Does that make sense?"

"Of course, Alf. I just wish you'd told me about this months ago. Have you talked about it with anyone else?"

"Sort of. Right before graduation in May, I went to my talk to my ROTC advisor, who is the professor of naval science in the Naval ROTC Department. I think I told you about him, didn't I? Anyway, he's a colonel in the Corps, a Citadel grad, and The Citadel is his final posting before retiring. He served in several hot spots that we've studied in ROTC, including with the 8th Marines in Grenada, Beirut, and other places where Marines got killed. I really trust his insights. His only son is actually in my class, but I haven't gotten to know him yet.

"So, I pretty much told him what I just told you, and it was the first time I'd verbalized all the mumbo-jumbo that was just in my head the last ten months and that I'd never shared with anyone until that afternoon.

"After listening to me, he stared across his desk and said, 'Can I tell you something, cadet? Since I met you back in August, I've seen much of myself from long ago in you, and now I see why. You worry too much about things you can't change. You need to find a way to focus on the things that you can possibly control or even change, if needed.'

"He then went on to talk about so-called enemies seen and unseen everywhere from The Citadel to Iraq. It was the first time that anyone had ever expressed it that way to me, including the military history I learned in ROTC. It definitely gave me a lot to think about in how I was dealing with things, and I'd hoped it might even help how I handled my time back here this summer, but so far I still feel like I'm in a funk and treating all of you so badly with my moods and silence."

"Quit thinking about us, Alf, and start thinking about yourself for once. Since August, we've all been afraid that holding it all in would eventually make you burst. It's talking about it with others that will help you get through this. Not keeping it inside and away from me and others."

"I know, Car. Mom was telling me the same thing last night. I can see the light at the end of the tunnel, and I just hope you're still there when I reach it."

"I will be, Alf. I will be." And I was.

BEN

———◆———

I NAIVELY HOPED that the summer after our freshman years could be a return to our summer idylls of the past, before Alf and Carolina became a couple and we all headed off to school. I'd even have been happy with a return to our summer before college, which would have at least given us back the Alf of old.

In some ways, that summer did have some similarities to summers past, in that the three of us pursued a few of the things we once loved about summers in the Upcountry. But whether eating ice cream at the Pickwick, where they only invited me to join them once, or going for a hike up on Paris Mountain, anything that involved Alf felt like we were all just going through the motions.

In July, after he completed his four-week ROTC commitment on the *Pensacola*, I decided to return to Edisto Island with Alf, Carolina, and her parents. Normally, we would have all ridden together in the Stones' Volvo wagon, but I must have known that it wouldn't go perfectly because I decided to drive our little '89 black VW bug. Alf rode beside me, and Carolina sat in the middle of the tiny back seat, leaning forward between our shoulders for much of the ride.

But I only lasted from one Saturday to the next before returning to Travelers Rest, while Mr. and Mrs. Stone, Carolina, and Alf stayed the traditional two weeks. I came back early for the same reason that I hadn't gone with them the previous summer, as well as a new one.

First and foremost, I still found it difficult to be around Alf and

Carolina as a couple and couldn't help wondering what it would have been like if Carolina had chosen me. I found myself feeling sorry for Carolina and thinking she would have been so much happier if she'd chosen me, and wondered whether she felt that way as well.

My brother was still making it difficult and awkward to be around him. He only spoke when one of us asked him a direct question, and he spent a lot of time just sitting out on the deck or down on the beach alone, staring at the Atlantic. When he was with one or more of us, his silences made everything about being there different and often depressing.

While the two of them stayed on the island with Carolina's parents, I made the drive back home alone, listening to a new Dixie Chicks CD I'd bought in Edisto. The album had a title track called "Wide Open Spaces," and I thought about Carolina when I heard lyrics like, "She needs wide open spaces. Room to make her big mistakes. She needs new faces. She knows the high stakes."

Long fond of wide-open spaces, was Car starting to think that returning Alf's seemingly stifling love was a big mistake? Did she know the high stakes? Did she need new faces? These were the thoughts of a boy desperate for earlier times, before the much higher stakes and big mistakes to come.

The week back home was a blessing in disguise. The air in our house somehow seemed lighter, and I didn't miss walking on eggshells or fighting my jealousy when I was with Alf and Carolina. My mother noticed it and, after I admitted to my feelings, said that she'd felt the same way after we'd left for the beach, and she could completely understand why I was having those thoughts.

Once the Stones, Carolina, and Alf returned to Travelers Rest, we only had three weeks left of summer break before we'd all head back for our second years. Though I knew my Third Class year as a "Rat with a radio" was going to be difficult in the classroom—it had been called the "Academic Ratline" for decades—I was ready to head back to VMI, where I'd already developed many friendships with classmates that I knew would last for a lifetime. And after thinking so much about Carolina that summer, I also looked forward to possibly getting to know Virginia better in the supposedly less stressful environment of our Third Class year.

I honestly hadn't thought too much about Virginia that summer; I'd barely gotten to know her Rat year. The administration discouraged and even forbid some relationships between cadets: we couldn't date someone in our chain of command. I was not going to hold rank as a corporal my Third Class year and didn't plan to pursue rank during my cadetship, but I wasn't sure if that was the case with Virginia.

ALF

————————— ■ —————————

AFTER MY TIME on board the *Pensacola*, where my commitment to service continued to grow, I hoped that a return to Edisto Island would work its magic on my mood, and the warm air and water did seem to soothe my frayed nerves. I spent a lot of time out on the deck or down on the beach, thinking about the past year at The Citadel and the year to come, as well as what life in the Marine Corps would hold for me—and Carolina. I was disappointed that Ben returned to TR after just one week on Edisto, but I understood his reasons.

If nothing else, I knew I wanted and needed to improve my moodiness and silences for sweet Carolina. She was being so incredibly patient with me and deserved better. I sometimes thought that, for her sake, she would have been better off picking Ben over me.

During our last Friday at the beach, Carolina and I went for a walk north toward the state park's beach, and after about five minutes of simply holding hands and saying nothing, I stared out to the ocean and quietly asked, "Do you ever wish you'd picked Ben instead of me, Car?"

She quickly stopped, pulling me back to her with some force. Though I tried to continue looking out to sea, Carolina took my chin in her other hand and made me look her in the eyes before saying, "I never want to hear that question or anything like it again, Alf. You're the one I chose, and I've never regretted it for a minute. I can't wait to see where our lives take us—together. What do the Marines say?

Semper fidelis, right? That's you and me. Always faithful."

I nodded, kept our gaze, and said, "Thank you, Car." And we turned back north—and toward a life that would test those words in ways we never could have imagined.

CAROLINA

I WAS STRANGELY glad that Alf had asked me whether I'd questioned my choice between him and Ben. I'd never thought twice about it until he went to The Citadel, and I could see that though they'd both gone to military colleges, my life with Alf was going to be very different than it would have been with Ben. Not better or worse, just different.

I'd thought about how I would respond to Alf if he ever asked me the question, and the idea of *semper fi* came to me after I heard him use the words with a Marine veteran at Whaley's one day.

That day, after Whaley's, when we were back in the car and driving to our beach house, I'd asked Alf what it meant and he'd said, "It's Latin for 'always faithful.' I think it's short for *semper fidelis*, and it seems to have lots of meanings, like always being faithful to your country and being faithful to your fellow Marines. Stuff like that."

"Do they use it at The Citadel?"

"Yeah. Mostly in Navy ROTC when Marine Corps cadets are talking to each other or with one of the Marine enlisted or officer instructors."

We rode the rest of the way back to the house in silence, but I remember thinking that day that those two Latin words would have many meanings for me in the years to come.

PART IV

BEN

———◆———

WE EACH HAD our unique reasons, but I think all three of us were ready for summer to end. I had a love-hate relationship with VMI that I learned was fairly typical with cadets and grads. The love part centered on doing something unique that you knew was pure and good, as well as a love of your brother Rats. The hate part had to do with all of the physical and mental strain that the VMI system places on you throughout your cadetship.

I was simply glad not to be a Rat as I watched them make their way to and from the fourth stoop in the Ratline, which already seemed both like a distant memory, yet something significant in my life that would never leave me. In any case, that August I found myself looking forward to a year at VMI that didn't involve the Ratline. Of course, that all changed the morning of September 11.

I will always remember where I was and what I was doing when I heard what had happened—and was happening—on September 11, 2001. I was in an English class in Scott Shipp Hall when the head of the department came in with an even more serious demeanor than he normally showed and said simply, "Classes are suspended, and everyone should report back to barracks."

Barracks was unusually and eerily quiet when I walked through Washington Arch. I asked a First leaning against the rail what was going on, and staring straight into the courtyard, he said, "Two planes hit both of those tall buildings at the World Trade Center.

Another one hit the Pentagon. And a fourth crashed somewhere in Pennsylvania. And all hell seems to be breaking loose in our country. I'd get up to your room."

I walked slowly up the third stoop without hearing another word spoken and found my two roommates already there, looking at a laptop and listening to someone speaking in a shaky tone.

I learned later that Laura, Virginia's dyke and mentor from the previous year, had been in the Pentagon visiting her father, who was on his last tour of duty with the Army before he and Laura's mom would retire in nearby Winchester. Even later, I'd learn that Virginia was given permission to go to her dyke's funeral up in Winchester later that week.

The next morning, after the strangest day I'd ever spend at VMI, in an ROTC class down the hill in Kilbourne Hall, an instructor told us that two VMI grads had also died on 9/11. Lieutenant Commander David Lucien Williams, Class of 1991, was killed at the Pentagon. Mr. Charles Mathers, Class of 1962, died at the World Trade Center. Since 9/11, more than a dozen VMI alumni have died while serving their country and fighting the global war on terrorism. Most of those deaths have occurred in Iraq, as well as Afghanistan.

More than any class could ever teach me, I learned that week that death and VMI are inevitably intertwined. So is service. Though fighting many new emotions, I was proud to be on the path to becoming part of a diverse group that still believes in the many manifestations of service to country.

CAROLINA

———○———

I REMEMBER EXACTLY where I was the morning of 9/11. I didn't have a class until the afternoon, so I'd slept in before getting up and going for a short run through town around eight thirty.

Usually, traffic in downtown Chapel Hill at that time of day would have been pretty heavy, but I still remember noticing as I ran back toward our apartment that there didn't seem to be any cars waiting at stoplights when I crossed over typically busy intersections like Franklin and Columbia, and where Columbia, North, and MLK came together. It wasn't until I'd returned to my apartment around nine and found my roommate, Lisa Dunn, intently watching TV, which was really unusual for her, that I sensed something was terribly wrong.

I closed our door and turned to her and the television to immediately hear her gasp and see the second plane hit. I remember saying, "Oh my God" through my hand while collapsing onto the couch beside her.

We'd only been rooming together for two weeks at that point, but that morning would bond us forever. We sat transfixed, arms around each other as the day progressed and the news got worse. I'm not sure I'll ever be able to process what happened that day—and how those damn planes and people who brought death to America would change my life and the lives of so many others forever.

ALF

—————■—————

I WAS IN my barracks room shining my shoes on the morning of 9/11 when an announcement came over the loudspeaker that everyone should report back to their barracks rooms.

Of course, I was among tens of millions who would soon realize their lives were forever changed that morning. Whether you lost a family member, a loved one, or knew someone who had, America was never the same after the bright sun rose on the East Coast that morning.

As soon as I'd heard about the World Trade Center and then the Pentagon and that field in Pennsylvania, I thought back to what my ROTC advisor had said about enemies in Iraq and other countries in that part of the world. I started seeing my future more clearly that day, located somewhere where the same blazing sun now in Charleston had already set in the sand.

I was glad to hear that no Citadel grads had died in New York, DC, or Pennsylvania on that bleak day—at least as far as anyone knew thus far. However, I wasn't naïve enough to believe that there would be no Citadel grad bloodshed in coming days, months, and even years. I knew that day that the blood could be that of my classmates—and even mine.

BEN

◆

THOUGH 9/11 WOULD never fade for any of us, time marched on, and the heat of summer seemed to fade quickly to cool fall mornings and evenings in Lexington, with the leaves on the trees around the Parade Ground changing to vibrant colors before falling to the ground to mark the start of another stark winter at the Institute, where you marched down to breakfast and supper in the dark.

Because we were in different companies and had different majors, I didn't see Virginia very often that fall. She was in New Barracks and I was rooming in Old Barracks again with three guys from my company, so barracks life and beyond were generally separated for Virginia and me.

One night in the fall, though, I asked Scott, a roommate from Richmond, what he thought about me asking Virginia to the homecoming dance. He said he thought it was a great idea, adding with a smile, "If you don't ask her, I will."

In the end, I couldn't and didn't pull the trigger. But I was glad Scott didn't either. I still felt like creating any complications or conflicts with girls while I was a cadet was a recipe for failure—especially because several of my classes that semester were definitely giving me trouble.

My mother didn't come up for any football games or for Parents Weekend that fall, so I went to the tailgate parties that the parents of my roommate, Jim Harris from Staunton, held before and after every football game. In November, the last home game was against East Tennessee, which we lost 41–23, ending the season with one win. While I was talking to Jim at his tailgate, I spotted Virginia walking across the Parade Ground with who I assumed was her mother and followed them to a Volvo station wagon parked closer to Moody Hall.

I watched as they joined a man who I would have figured was Virginia's dad had I not known he had died when she was young; she hugged him, as well as an older couple with whom Virginia also shared lingering hugs. "Hey, roomie," Jim said, punching me in the arm. "Why don't you quit staring and drooling, and just walk over there and talk to our brother Rat. That's Virginia, right?"

I laughed nervously, replying, "Yeah, that's her. That must be her family. I can't just waltz over there and ask for a burger, can I?"

"Nah. I'd go for the steak it looks like her father is grilling," he joked. "That's some serious tailgating goin' on over there. It makes my parents' hot dogs and chips look pretty lame, huh?"

"Well, you know I'll take anything over mess hall food, BR, and your parents are so great to let me eat with y'all. But I do think I'll head over there just to say hey."

"Good luck, Ben," he said, mockingly pushing me in their direction. "The worst thing she can do is tell you to get lost. Or maybe her father will do it for her."

I walked slowly over to their car and tent, which was flying a 1984 VMI flag on one corner post and a red, white, and yellow one with "64" on it attached to another corner post. Virginia looked up from a conversation when I was about ten feet away and smiled, waving me over.

"Hey, Ben. I thought that was you. How's Third Class life in Old Barracks treating you?" she asked, not waiting for an answer before saying, "Oh, hey, Ben, this is my father's best friend, Nick Adams. He's Class of '84, just like my dad."

"It's great to meet you, Ben," said Mr. Adams, holding out his ring-laden hand. "How's it going for you here? I know it can be a pretty rough place at times."

"It's going fine, sir," I said, registering his firm handshake and the way he seemed to hold eye contact with me a beat longer than seemed comfortable. "The classes seem a lot harder this year than Rat year. Did they call it the Academic Ratline when you were here, sir?"

"Yep, they sure did, Ben. I was roommates with Virginia's dad, Chip, and, man, did he have it hard. I was an English major, so it wasn't too bad. But he was a chemistry nerd, wasn't he, Ginny? I swear he did nothing but study that year."

"That's what y'all tell me," said Virginia, not taking her eyes off him. "That's why I'm majoring in English too. VMI's tough enough without failing classes and having to come back here for summer school. Did Dad, you, or Uncle Bradley ever come back for summer school, Uncle Nick?"

"Just Bradley came back for summer school, Gin," said Mr. Adams, before gesturing to Virginia and turning to me and continuing. "This Rat with a radio here is probably leaving you in the dark about who's who, huh, Ben?"

"Yes sir. I'm afraid so, Mr. Adams."

"Well, let's start with you calling me Nick. Then, here's a rundown on who's who here," he continued, his ring glinting in the sun as he waved his right hand at the small group before us.

"I was lucky enough to be roommates with Chip our Rat year back in '80 and '81, and the following three years back in barracks over there—same room, down a stoop each year. Her dad changed my life. I'm not really Virginia's uncle, but I guess I've been like one to her from the day she was born. But that's another story, like me writing travel and food stories for a living.

"The Uncle Bradley that Virginia just mentioned when she asked about us going to summer school was our other roommate those long four years. His name is Bradley Bell, and it's very likely you'll meet him here or maybe down in Beaufort—the one in South Carolina—sometime.

"Bradley was from Charleston and a family full of Citadel grads," he continued. "But that's another story too. That couple over there are Win and Sarah Shields, and they're Chip's parents. They're talking to Ginny's lovely mom, Beth. Win is Class of 1964. True Old Corps. Which I'm not—yet. I'll introduce you to all of 'em in a minute. Make sense, Ben?"

"Yes sir. So far."

Mr. Adams quietly added, "And for full disclosure, we lost Gin's dad a long time ago, Ben, but it seems like yesterday that I was on this Parade Ground with him and his parents. I miss him terribly, but especially when I'm here."

"I do too, Uncle Nick," Virginia said with a crack in her voice. "Every day. But especially late at night in barracks. I sometimes sleep with his ring on my middle finger. He had small hands, and it almost fits."

"We got the exact same ring," said Mr. Adams, holding up his big ring to Virginia and then me. "Hey, let's go look at Win's ring, you two. It's not too long that you'll both be getting your own rings, huh?"

Meeting Nick Adams and Virginia's family on that cool fall day was one of those times at VMI that I'll always remember. They made me feel like I was part of a family and fraternity in a way that I'd always heard bonded the VMI family, no matter what their connection to the Institute.

Though I was guessing he must have been in his sixties or seventies after doing some quick math, Win Shields stood upright, as if at attention, and shook hands with me like he meant it. Like Nick, he also locked eyes with me a beat longer than normal. I felt like he was trying to tell me something.

Sarah Shields was an elegant bookend to Mr. Shields, with long gray hair and sparkling blue eyes that shimmered in the morning sun when she smiled. As Win Shields and Nick Adams exchanged stories about their time at VMI and Virginia chimed in occasionally with a story of her own, it was obvious Mrs. Shields had heard them all before, as we occasionally exchanged smiles and knowing nods.

Virginia's mom, Beth, was equally beautiful, but in a different way. The first thing I noticed were her eyes, which were gray, exactly like Virginia's. She also had blond hair like Virginia but wore it longer. I wondered that day what Virginia's hair would look like if she grew it long like her mom's.

It seemed like I'd been at their tailgate for a few minutes when I glanced at my watch and realized I'd been away from my roommate's tailgate for a half hour. I awkwardly said some quick goodbyes to everyone except Virginia and Mr. Adams, who were talking quietly, and made my way back to my roommate and his parents in somewhat of a fog about the people I'd just met. Over the years to come, that fog would clear, and I would grow to love each of them with all of my heart.

As I was walking away from their tailgate, I suddenly found it odd that 9/11 had never come up in conversation like it had practically anytime people gathered that fall. Considering what I learned later about Laura and her dad being killed on that September morning, they were likely avoiding the topic.

A couple of weeks after the final fall football game and my brief time with Virginia and her extended family, I was sitting in my barracks room shooting the breeze with my roommates right before taps, and over a Dave Matthews song we heard a confident knock on our worn wooden door. It was Virginia asking for permission to enter our all-male room, in case we weren't fully clothed.

Seeming more nervous and less confident than I'd seen her during our other admittedly brief encounters, Virginia entered, walked over to my desk, and said, "I just got a note from my mom that she and Uncle Nick want to drive over from Richmond to take me to brunch Sunday morning. And she asked me to see if you wanted to go with us."

Behind Virginia, a roommate, Dave, started making lewd gestures with his hands, distracting me enough to falter and awkwardly respond, "Um, sure."

Noticing me glancing around her, Virginia quickly turned around but didn't catch my roommate in the act. She turned back to me and hesitated before simply saying, "Great, Ben. Why don't we meet in front of Jackson Statue at oh nine thirty? You're not on confinement or anything, right?"

I quickly said, "No" as she turned and headed for the door. She probably saw me flipping Dave the bird in the reflection of one of the door's paneled windows, but she didn't break stride. I'd be remiss by not saying that she looked darned good in her uniform as she walked across our little room toward a door that thankfully hadn't been kicked in too many times to count like our door last year on the stoop above.

We didn't have breakfast formation on Sunday mornings, so we got to sleep in. All of my roommates were asleep when I slipped out of our room in my blouse. After exiting Jackson Arch, I saw the three of them waiting for me in front of Jackson's towering statue. I was surprised that Mrs. Shields gave me a quick hug, with a smiling Nick going for the firm handshake and that still somewhat strange and awkward locking-of-eyes thing they did.

I sat in the back seat of Nick's green Volvo wagon, with Virginia sitting across from me, behind her mom, who sat half turned in the front seat to share stories and ask both Virginia and me questions during the drive.

"I talked Nick into taking the Blue Ridge Parkway back down to Peaks of Otter," Mrs. Shields said as we headed down the little Letcher Avenue hill through W&L and downtown and then passed the Hampton Inn on Route 60. The highway heads east out of Lexington and parallels the Maury River for much of the short drive to Buena Vista. "We took Virginia there during Parents Weekend last year, and we thought you'd really enjoy it as well, Ben. It's a special place. Especially to the Shields family. And that includes Nick."

As we passed through what I now called "BV," Nick glanced in in his rearview mirror and told us about the all-female, two-year school on the hill that they once called "Southern See-menary" instead of Southern Seminary. "Evidently some of the girls back then were pretty loose," he said. "At least according to my brother Rats. It's now a very pretty four-year, religious-based school that belies its former debauchery—at least according to some males." While Nick was talking, gazing at me in the rearview mirror, Virginia and her mom kept shaking their heads and smiling, like they'd heard this tale previously, which I guess they had.

About five miles on the other side of BV, we headed up onto the Blue Ridge Parkway, with Nick saying, "I still love this road" as we turned right to start the drive south.

"Oh, you love any road, Nick," said Mrs. Shields, smiling at him with obvious affection. "Especially if it leads to a restaurant."

"I once happily took any road that led me away from VMI, but now that Miss Virginia's there, I feel differently. Especially if there's a meal involved that's most definitely not in the mess hall."

"Well, this road right here is leading down memory lane to a pretty darn good brunch, Ben," said Mrs. Shields. "As I mentioned, we actually brought Gin here last year, and it was quite the march down memory lane for all of us, as y'all like to say. Though Gin didn't remember the first time she was at Peaks of Otter.

"I was just thinking about it this morning over my first cup of that good Hampton Inn coffee out on my balcony," Mrs. Shields continued. "Until our trip down here, we hadn't been this way since the spring of 1984, when Virginia was just a toddler. She was born while her dad was still a cadet, Ben."

Turning to me, Virginia said, "I didn't know this story until they brought me here last month."

Nick continued the thread, saying, "Gin's grandparents brought Virginia and her mom here from Richmond and stayed in Lexington, while the four—I mean five—of us drove down here. I think we even took the Parkway that time as well. I was already into road trips even back then."

"I can't believe y'all took the chance bringing Mom and me along when it meant that if Dad got caught, he might get kicked out of VMI just before graduation."

"We'd all grown a bit gutsier by then," said Nick. "We never went out together in town that semester, but we occasionally did trips like this that last semester and only had one close call."

"What was the close call?" I asked as Nick veered his wagon into a pull-off just before the James River. A sign indicated that, at just 649 feet, it was the lowest point on the entire Parkway.

The four of us got out of the car and went to sit on one of the many stone fences along the Parkway. "So, tell me about the close call, y'all," I insisted.

"I'm surprised Virginia hasn't already shared this story with you, Ben," Nick said, smiling as he thought back to something that must have happened about twenty years ago. "But maybe she was waiting for her mom and me to be here as well. Anyway, I swear I think her dad, Chip, may actually have packed his duffel bag that time."

"Can I try telling it, Uncle Nick?" Virginia asked, receiving a nod from Nick to continue. "It's funny how it doesn't sound like a big deal now, but it evidently sure could have been.

"You see, Ben," Virginia continued, holding my gaze, "my dad occasionally met me and my mom and my grandparents somewhere between Lexington and Richmond where it was unlikely I'd be seen. Uncle Nick, and Uncle Bradley as well, sometimes joined us. They thought there'd be strength in numbers and that most people would assume that my mom and I were the sister and niece of one of them. You do know that you can't be married or have a child while you're a cadet at VMI, right, Ben?"

"Okay, my turn, slowpoke," said Nick after I'd nodded to Virginia that I knew that rule about marriage and children. "No offense, Gin, but I get paid to tell stories," Nick continued.

"Only if they involve food," Mrs. Shields retorted. "But I guess this one does in the end."

"Yeah, I guess it does involve eating in the end, doesn't it?" Nick said, laughing while staring down at the slow-moving James River below us. "Many of my stories do. Anyway, Ben, one April day,

Gin's dad, her so-called Uncle Bradley, and I had driven up 81 from Lexington to Edelweiss in Raphine for some really good German food and beer. Virginia's grandparents planned to meet us there with her and her mom. By the way, we need to take you there sometime, you two. They have very good German grub. And tasty Deutschland wines and beers as well.

"Anyway, we got there, and y'all were already inside," Nick continued. "Virginia's dad went straight to Gin and gave her an exaggerated kiss on the top of her head before shaking hands with Win, his father, and hugging Win's wife, Sarah, Gin's grandmother, as well as Beth here, of course." He pointed at Mrs. Shields. "We were behind your dad at the time, so we had seen the deputy commandant in civilian clothes sitting at a corner table with his wife. Your dad hadn't noticed him yet."

"Did you freak out, Mrs. Shields?" I asked.

"It didn't really hit me at first that it could be a very big deal," she quietly said, seemingly lost in the memory. "Virginia's dad and grandfather, plus her two uncles, went over to the table to say hello, leaving the three of us back at our table. The officer and his wife were just finishing lunch, and after they left, we proceeded to play out all of the mostly bad scenarios that could happen. No one was in a mood to eat or drink much—even Nick here, who always seems hungry and thirsty."

"That's me," said Nick, still looking down at the river and lost in the memory of that long-ago day. "I remember it was an unusually quiet meal for this crowd. Gin's mom and grandparents then headed back to Richmond, and we came back to barracks in her dad's eerily and unusually quiet car.

"We didn't hear anything the rest of that day or Sunday, but Gin's dad got a message slip Monday morning telling him to report to the deputy commandant's office at thirteen hundred that afternoon. We were waiting in our room when he got back just a couple of minutes after one with a completely blank expression."

Nick got up from the rock fence, walked to the ledge of the overlook, and turned back to us to say, "Chip sat on his cot and told us that the deputy commandant had called him into his office and, after returning your dad's salute, simply asked if it was his wife and child he'd seen at the restaurant Saturday."

Beth Shields picked up the thread of the story, saying, "I think Chip had thought about how he'd answer a direct question like that many times since we'd gotten married and Virginia was born, so he was prepared with a quick answer."

"'Yes, sir. That's correct, sir.' That's exactly what Chip said was his response that afternoon," Nick continued, shaking his head at the memory.

"Then, the deputy commandant—I think his name was Snider or something like that—said, 'That is all' and dismissed Chip. He couldn't have been gone three minutes. We were just down the stoop from his office.

"The three of us sat around and talked about it for most of the afternoon," Nick continued. "Sorta like we are now, but not with this great view. We just assumed the deputy commandant was going to tell the higher-ups and your dad would never graduate from VMI after keeping it a secret for so long. But y'all already know that wasn't the case."

"So, what happened?" I asked.

"Chip didn't even tell me about any of this until after graduation," said Mrs. Shields. "I was honestly scared to ask until then. I guess it's anticlimactic in retrospect, but the end of this story really is that nothing happened. Chip kept waiting to get summoned to the supe's office at Smith Hall across the Parade Ground, but it just never happened."

Nick continued with, "We didn't talk about it much that spring and just assumed the deputy commandant was going through the proper channels to confirm the marriage—and Virginia's existence," said Nick. "But come May and graduation, Chip walked across the stage to get his diploma just like the rest of us—except he had a wife and child sitting in the audience. Little did he know, Gin, that you'd walk across that stage one day as well. We'll all be there for you, you know. And you too, Ben."

"Wow," I exclaimed. "Did anyone ever ask this Snider guy why he never did anything?"

"I still believe that Chip was afraid they might still be able to do something even after graduation," said Nick. "We all wanted to let sleeping dogs lie, so to speak. I think Snider stayed at VMI for another five years or so, but I have no idea where he is now.

"In a weird way, I think it was an honorable thing that Snider did," Nick continued. "Chip never said this, but I believe he thought that Snider had decided Chip had done the right thing by marrying Beth—and by answering the direct question from him with the only reply he'd decided he could provide."

"What a story, y'all," I said.

"There are lots more of them we'd love to share with you over time, Ben," said Mrs. Shields. "We went through a lot back then and in the years to come. In many ways, Virginia's cadetship is creating a new stage in our lives, and a new round of stories you two will likely be sharing with other loved ones someday," said Mrs. Shields, looking to Virginia and me in turn.

"Okay, you three," said Nick. "This talk about Edelweiss has made me hungry. Let's get going before they run out of food at Peaks of Otter."

When we arrived at the parking lot in front of the main lodge, we found that the restaurant wasn't very full yet, so we were able to get a table by the window overlooking the lake. "This is sorta surreal," Mrs. Shields said. "This is the third straight time they've seated us at this table."

"How do you remember this stuff, Mom?" asked Virginia.

"I know," said Mrs. Shields. "Nick's usually the one who remembers all of his meals, including where he ate, who he ate with, and even every single dish they ordered."

"Of course I remember sitting right here those other two times, y'all," said Nick, smiling at me. "The first time, back in '84, I kept feeding Virginia bites of ham from the buffet, and she loved it."

"I still do, Uncle Nick," Virginia said, smiling. "And I noticed a big pile of ham slices up at the buffet with my name on it."

We ordered iced tea with our various preferences for sweeteners, then the four of us went up to the buffet, which we had to ourselves. Virginia pointed to the little "Virginia Cured Ham" placard placed above the pile of slices and said, "See? The ham really did have my name on it."

"And that's going to be my appetizer," said Nick, grinning and filling his plate with ham and a couple of oversized biscuits. I saw him stop to talk to the waitress and figured he was probably asking them to bring out a new batch of fried chicken so it would be hot and crisp. I later learned that Nick often did stuff like that at restaurants and even made special toppings requests for his burgers at McDonald's so the beef patties would be fresh off their greasy griddles. I liked that even a gourmet like Nick went to McDonald's occasionally, claiming they had some of the best French fries anywhere, including France.

Mrs. Shields, Virginia, and I spent more time up at the buffet, adding the typical Southern appetizers of mixed salad and still-warm bread to our plates. Back at the table, the waitress I'd seen Nick talking to was uncorking a bottle of white wine, which I surmised was the reason for their earlier conversation.

"I hope a light dry German Riesling is okay for whoever's drinking. I figured it would work with ham, chicken, or whatever else we had. Feel free to get something else, y'all, if you'd prefer."

Mrs. Shields and Virginia said they'd have a glass, so I said yes as well. I really didn't know much about wine, and that day at Peaks of Otter marked the beginning of my wine education by Nick, with Virginia joining his classroom as well.

After he'd poured wine into each of our glasses, Nick asked, "Can we toast Chip?"

"Why, sure," said Mrs. Shields, raising her glass and nodding at me to raise mine.

Nick then said, "To a brother Rat, friend, husband, and father," and the four of us clinked glasses, with Nick going through that locked-eyes thing with Mrs. Shields and Virginia, before turning to me, locking eyes, and clinking my glass.

"So, I gotta ask," I said, looking at Nick. "What's the deal with the locked eyes when y'all shake hands, hug, toast, and stuff?"

Nick laughed and said, "Yeah, I sometimes forget how weird it may seem to people. Chip actually started it with Bradley and me back in the fall of our Rat year. We'd noticed that, at tailgates, when he and Win Shields shook hands, they'd hold their grip and eyes for several seconds more than seemed normal.

"When Chip would see us again, even after a short separation, he did the same with both of us. I guess we've all simply tried to carry on the tradition."

Virginia nodded, saying, "Since my dad died, all of y'all have tried so hard to fill the huge hole he left. Don't think I haven't noticed and appreciated it. I've missed sharing VMI with him, but all of you have helped with that as well."

"We miss him too, honey," said Mrs. Shields, looking down at her plate. "I'd give anything to have him walking up to the table right now with a big plate of fried chicken."

"He could eat some chicken, couldn't he, Mom?" asked Virginia.

Before she could answer, Nick said, "In many ways, Chip and his parents introduced me to good food—especially this Southern stuff—and I guess it eventually led to this crazy and quite fattening career of mine."

"I always thought it was ironic that Chip never got fat or had high blood pressure or bad cholesterol numbers," Mrs. Shields said. "He ate like Stonewall Jackson's horse. It was one of his life's many ironies that he died of a cancer he didn't cause instead of a heart attack from eating all of that unhealthy food."

"Well, if I keep eating all of this sweet Southern cooking and reviewing all of those restaurants for Michelin and other places, I'll be the one having a heart attack." Nick mugged like a glutton, holding up a chicken drumstick to make his point. "But I'll die fat and happy."

"All of you need to stay healthy, Uncle Nick," said Virginia. "If Dad can't be at our graduation, the two of you better be. They'll all be there for you too, Ben."

"That's a promise, you two," said Nick. "Who would have thought that you'd be in the audience at Cameron Hall for your dad's graduation, Gin, and then walk across that same stage some twenty or so years later?"

"That's a few years from now for sure, but I plan to be there and have you two in the audience. Oh, and Grandma and Granddad too. I wish they could have come this weekend."

"You know they would have been here if they felt up to the trip," said Nick. "They brought us up here a few times during our cadetships."

"I'm still amazed how little I know about my other grandparents," said Virginia. "But Grandma and Granddad make up for that."

"They sure do, honey," said Mrs. Shields, looking at Virginia. "They welcomed me from the day I met them, and we couldn't have asked for more of them after your dad died and they were experiencing their own heartbreaking grief."

Nick stood and nodded toward the buffet, saying, "And speaking of Chip and his affection for Southern food, I'm going back for some of that fried chicken." The three of us exchanged smiles as he made his way back to the food.

"That's an amazing man," said Virginia.

"Yeah. I don't know what we would have done without him before and after your dad died. He dropped everything to be in Richmond, and I know he missed several big writing assignments—and meals— to be with us.

"I sometimes wish he'd talk more about your dad, like today," Mrs.

Shields continued, looking at Nick up at the buffet. "He just told me recently that he held your dad's head over a cracked MCV toilet many times during his chemo, and they joked that they were more than blood brothers—they were brothers in bile. Like me, he changed those diapers your dad had to wear near the end. He says he gets knots in his stomach every time he thinks about all of us losing him."

"Me too," Virginia said, following her gaze. "It was bad enough back home in Richmond, but it's even worse sometimes at VMI. I feel like he's watching me in the Ratline, and I guess that's a good thing, but I miss being able to share this time with him so much."

"I know, honey. He would have smiled at the thought of you in that blouse, but he'd also be glad Nick has been here for you."

Nick came back with a plate of a half dozen pieces of chicken for the table to share, as well as another large plate of varied desserts. Nick and I each grabbed a piece of chicken, while Virginia and Mrs. Shields shared a slice of cheesecake. We spent the next half hour sharing more VMI stories separated by two decades and a dead father, husband, and best friend.

I think it was at this lunch that Nick shared another tale. This one was about the mysterious Bradley Bell. Though I didn't recall it, Nick said he'd briefly mentioned Bradley to me when we first met, saying at the time that it was yet another story. And it was.

Nick reminded me that he, Virginia's dad, and Bradley roomed together all four years at VMI, moving straight down to the room below each successive year. He said that Bradley's father and brother were both Citadel grads, and they'd both essentially disowned him as a son and brother when he'd chosen VMI over The Citadel.

"Bradley's dad was a jerk," Nick said, almost spitting the words. "Ironically, he's the only Citadel grad I've met in all these years that I didn't like. There's a certain camaraderie between VMI and Citadel grads that I think you'll find in years to come, Ben and Virginia. Anyway, Bradley's jerk of a dad ran a clothing store that his father had started on King Street back in Charleston. Bradley's older brother graduated from The Citadel and went right to work for dear old dad. I only saw Bradley's father once, which was the day we graduated. It was quite the day in so many ways, which I'll explain.

"So, besides us—and his mom, sometimes, I guess—Bradley had no support at VMI. But he made it through, while keeping an amazing secret, which he didn't share with me, Gin's dad, or anyone else until graduation day. That was the day he told us he was gay."

"Wow," I said. "That's pretty amazing, huh? You didn't have any idea, Nick?"

"Nope," Nick said, shaking his head for emphasis. "I don't think any of us had an inkling. Of course, that was during the 'Don't ask, don't tell' policy period in the military, but still. It took a strong will to make it through VMI in the best of cases, but having to keep your sexual identity a secret? After graduation and serving in the Navy, where they didn't ask and Bradley didn't tell, he opened a great men's clothing store down in Beaufort, just an hour or so down Route 17 from Charleston. It's sorta like Alvin-Dennis in Lexington.

"Bradley never really reconciled with his father, who I heard died a few years back, or his brother, who still lives in Charleston, I think, even though their store shut down. I like to believe that Bradley's Beaufort shop took all of their customers. Anyway, I hope you meet good ole Bradley here or down in Beaufort."

I did indeed meet Bradley on the Parade Field the following fall and, after graduation, made my way to the pretty riverfront town of Beaufort to visit him and his shop. I love a pale-blue sweater I bought there that day and wear it often. Bradley calls it Citadel blue, which makes me smile.

After lunch and all of those still-fresh stories, the four of us walked around the little lake behind Peaks of Otter, pausing several times in the woods on the opposite bank to glance back at the old hotel and restaurant. I still love that view. And those people.

We got back from our memorable road trip late in the afternoon because Nick insisted that we take the Blue Ridge Parkway back, with

Mrs. Shields and Nick switching seats because he'd had three glasses of wine to her one. The three of them continued to trade Shields family stories, and I just soaked it all up, relishing their obvious affection for each other and for Chip Shields, who was already feeling like a formidable presence in my life.

They dropped Virginia and me off at Jackson Arch, and it would be the first of many times I'd say goodbye to one or more of them in front of that iconic statue.

ALF

MY SECOND YEAR at The Citadel was, of course, marked by September 11. Most Americans, and especially those at military schools or already serving, marked time by pre-9/11 and post-9/11. We simply could not have predicted how those terrorist acts would lead to destinies we never fathomed before that day.

After the initial shock of 9/11, we had to soldier on as cadets in this new world, and my second year at The Citadel was, in many ways, strangely less stressful. Certainly, not having the constant pressures of being a Knob made my time inside and outside of barracks less trying, but I had also learned to better manage my time and prioritize.

That fall, I found myself not taking things that happened at The Citadel so seriously. Actually, I was learning what to take seriously and what not to, and that very few things at The Citadel—and maybe in life—were worth stressing over. Of course, it helped that a certain cadet had graduated that spring.

The Marine Corps advisor I'd met with twice the previous May, just before graduation, seemed to notice this change and commented on it during our first advisory meeting in September, saying, "You seem to be more relaxed this fall, Cadet Marshall. Why do you think that is?"

"I agree, sir," I responded. "I think it's just a function of getting used to the system and realizing that not everything—actually, very little—is life and death. I also think I'm less stressed about that matter I shared with you last May."

"That's a ten-four on both observations, cadet. The sooner you learn and use that knowledge, the better you'll do in this place. And in life. But do remember that down here in the ROTC Department, much of what we're doing actually does involve life and death."

"Yes sir," I said, thinking about the battles we'd been studying, and the lives lost. "Did you ever lose any of your men, sir?"

He stared out his window toward Wilson Field for a few seconds, before returning his gaze across his desk to me, saying, "Of course, cadet. There aren't too many Corps officers and enlisted men serving here now who haven't lost brothers-in-arms. The Corps' involvement in the Persian Gulf and beyond was so heavy, as you know, that I lost several men in my company and battalion."

"We're studying some of those battles now, sir."

"Well, I'd pay close attention, because I believe the Marine Corps will be back in that area someday fighting who knows what or who."

I wasn't sure how to respond when he added, still gazing out the window, "And the heat. Always, the heat."

I had to leave for my next class at that point, but I would think about his comments many times in coming days, months, and—eventually—years.

CAROLINA

———○———

AFTER THE SHOCK of 9/11 and what I knew it might mean for Alf—and Ben—I had to continue my life in Chapel Hill as best as possible. But life and death for me and so many others would never be the same after that morning.

Though under the deep shadow of 9/11 every day, my second year at Chapel Hill was, in most ways, even better than my first year there. Like the previous spring when I'd really started coming into my own on and off campus, those fall days were a blur of classes, studying, lots of sorority stuff, and my work on *The Daily Tar Heel*. My life back in Travelers Rest, as well as Alf's struggles, seemed to fade as September turned to October.

I did feel that Alf's moodiness had improved somewhat when I visited him for a weekend in September. I caught a ride with a Tri Sig sister who happened to be from Chapel Hill and had a car at home she could borrow. She was visiting her childhood sweetheart, who was a sophomore at the College of Charleston, so she gave me a ride.

Unlike my earlier visit to The Citadel with Alf's mom the previous fall, it was just Alf and me this time. I'm not sure that this was the reason that Alf seemed to be in a better mood, but me being me, I just asked him, "You don't seem quite as stressed out, Alf. Is it because your mom's not here this time?"

We were walking along Lee Avenue, and he nodded across Summerall Field toward Padgett-Thomas Barracks and said, "It's not

Mom not being here, Car. I think I'm just handling life in barracks and beyond much better this year and not taking stuff so seriously. At least, not the stuff that doesn't matter in the big picture. Like perfectly shined shoes or a rifle you could put in your mouth and not worry about germs. Not that I would," he continued, turning to me and smiling.

"Well, that's good," I said, returning his smile and grabbing his hand, which he quickly pulled away before speaking.

"Don't forget we're not allowed any public displays of affection on campus, Car."

"Oops. Sorry. I guess I forgot."

"No prob. I just don't want to get demerits or worse just for a few seconds of holding hands with you," he said, suddenly more serious than seemed warranted.

There was a hint of the old tension in his voice and jaw, but it evaporated as quickly as it had appeared. "I'm just glad to see you not taking all of the rules and other stuff here too seriously, Alf."

"I'm trying." And he did, generally.

Alf and I never became one of those couples who always held hands when they were together. He just didn't seem interested in showing his affection for me that way or in other ways our friends often did when we were together back in TR, like putting their arms around each other or casually kissing. It wasn't Alf's way.

That September visit was the first of several that fall that really ignited a love affair with Charleston that I've never lost, even with all that would happen. I particularly enjoyed Sunday mornings, when I would meet Alf outside barracks and we would stroll downtown, enjoying the architecture and gardens north and south of Broad before finding a restaurant for brunch or lunch. For the next few years, we devoted ourselves to discovering the best shrimp and grits in town, as well as other classic Southern dishes like she-crab soup. Where most couples had their songs, Alf and I had our dishes—the shrimp and grits at Slightly North of Broad and she-crab soup at 82 Queen.

Though I still sometimes questioned his choice to attend The Citadel and pursue a commission in the Marine Corps, I was starting to see some light at the end of the tunnel.

BEN

———◆———

MY ROOMMATES AND other classmates claimed taking Virginia to our Ring Figure ceremony was like taking your sister, but I paid them no heed, and neither did Virginia. We were still just friends and classmates, though I now look back and can see that, by that November weekend, our relationship had evolved.

However, for Ring Figure weekend, we were just two brother Rats and friends who could share one of VMI's very special moments. Unless your date, male or female, was—or had been—a cadet, there was no way for her or him to understand the significance of the VMI ring.

There's not much to say about the weekend, beyond that it was the second happiest day I would spend at the Institute—the first remains graduation day. My third best day at the Institute was Breakout. There were some other good days—and, of course, some tough ones as well.

It was definitely strange standing in that huge ring replica and having Virginia put that iconic ring on my finger. Like Nick and her grandfather would likely have done as well, she locked eyes with me as she slipped it on my finger. I then returned the honor and privilege with her. We both joked later that night that it was almost like getting married.

That evening, Virginia and I danced together for the first time. Although we also danced with other classmates, and the dates of classmates we knew wouldn't mind, Virginia and I always found each other for the slow songs.

At the party that Saturday night, Virginia told me she'd planned a surprise for me the next day. Because of the loud music, she'd had to say it right into my ear before leaning back and grinning. I looked at her with quizzical eyes, wondering what it could be, but she simply kept smiling without saying another word.

My surprise was waiting outside barracks the next morning at ten sharp when I headed out of Jackson Arch, as Virginia had requested. There, in the late-morning shadow of Jackson Statue, my mother, Virginia's mom, and Nick Adams stood waiting with Virginia, who was beaming.

Shaking my head in disbelief and happiness, I walked up to them, saying as I approached, "What a great way to end this weekend, y'all." I gave my mother a long hug and shook Nick's hand, noticing how much heavier my right hand felt, now newly ring-clad like Nick's.

"Congratulations, Ben," Mom, Mrs. Shields, and Nick said, almost in unison.

"Thanks, y'all, and thank you, Virginia, for somehow getting my mom here to surprise me."

"It was actually my mother's great idea to track down your mom, and, naturally, it didn't take much convincing when I called her."

"I'd been thinking about driving up here to surprise you, but it took Virginia's call to convince me. I hope you're pleased, Ben."

"Oh, more than you can know, Mom. Sharing this weekend with Virginia has been amazing. But now, getting to show you my ring—and y'all too, Nick and Mrs. Shields—is icing on the cake."

"That's great, son." Taking my right hand in both of hers and admiring my ring, she said, "I can't believe how big it is, Ben."

"I know, Mom. You see them on Seconds and Firsts—and grads like Nick—but you somehow can't picture one on your own finger. Until this weekend, that is. Right, Virginia?"

Nick jumped in, saying, "I know what you mean, Ben," looking back and forth between me and Virginia like he was noticing something for the first time. "The three of us now share a bond that goes way beyond these big chunks of gold on our fingers. We have common VMI experiences that haven't changed much over the decades, and we share something special that isn't based on when you graduated or how you performed at the Institute. When you have a VMI ring—and diploma, in my opinion—you have bonds unlike those from any other college in the country."

"Well said, Uncle Nick." Virginia chuckled. "You must be a writer or something."

"You know I can't turn it off, y'all," retorted Nick, looking down at his worn ring. "This place—and this ring—really get me going. And speaking of going, how 'bout we get going to brunch somewhere?"

Like much of the weekend, brunch passed in a blur. I think we went to the Southern Inn. I have to ask Virginia sometime if that's where we dined that day.

Another thing I will always remember about that fall are the essays that Alf and I had to write, though it wouldn't be until Christmas that we learned of the coincidence concerning our chosen topics. My essay was for my history class, where we were assigned to write no more than five hundred words about war. We'd been studying several key Civil War battles—and their horrors—so I'd been thinking a lot about the stupidity of war. While my brother Rats chose topics like Jackson's loss of an arm at Chancellorsville, and Lee's Appomattox surrender to Grant, I chose the unique topic of "the end of war." I found the essay in a box from my days at VMI that hadn't been opened in years.

THE END OF WAR
by Ben Marshall

As with many good things that happen in this world, it all began with a woman. A mom. She was the mother of a soldier who died in yet another war in yet another war-torn country thousands of miles from the place he'd called home for all but six months of his all too short life.

The mother was an Army brat who was determined that her son would know only one home in his childhood. And she'd succeeded until the day he enlisted in the Marine Corps.

Her husband had enlisted in the Corps right after those planes hit the World Trade Center, the Pentagon, and that sacred field in Pennsylvania. He'd deployed four times and had returned with medals and memories that he'd filed away for what he thought would be forever. Until their son enlisted exactly twenty years to the day after those planes and people changed the world forever.

The son chose the Marine Corps like his father, and he reported to Parris Island late in the fall of 2041. His father drove him. His mother didn't, or couldn't, make the trip. But his mother did attend graduation thirteen long weeks later, staying in a cheap roadside hotel in Beaufort that her husband found on the internet the day the boy learned when he'd report to—and graduate from—Parris Island.

After his ten days of traditional "boot leave" back home, the son next went to Camp Lejeune's Camp Geiger for Marine Combat Training. The additional training had a purpose—to get him ready for war and killing in who knew where. There were many possibilities that winter.

The mother was the one who opened the door six months later. A Marine Corps captain and chaplain awaited with the news she knew before they set foot inside the little house. She fell into the stunned officer's broad chest and wept the tears of tens of thousands of mothers across the centuries.

The father would soon have a second set of medals and memories to file. But the wife, the mother, the woman wouldn't let her husband keep them in the closet, like his mementoes.

She put their son's boxed flag on their coffee table the

day she received it from the Marine Corps, and she touched it every morning before she went to their kitchen table and did what she was destined to do. Morning by morning, she worked to end war—everywhere.

The son lived on through his mother's years-long efforts to end war. And it actually happened, because one mother and then another, and another, and then millions of mothers started to say "No more war" to the men, mostly, who'd made war for centuries. They said no in ballot boxes, in places of worship, at kitchen tables, in bedrooms, and, most importantly, on the internet.

In the end, on September 11, 2051, almost ten years after the son's death, every country in the world signed a United Nations proclamation that was simply called "The End of War." It seemed appropriate that a body founded in 1945, just after World War II ended but well before many more, to end the scourge of war for future generations would achieve just that. And it all started with a mother.

My history professor singled out the essay in front of the class the following week, saying he was giving me an A minus. He said the A was for my creativity, adding that it was the first time in his three years of giving that particular essay assignment that anyone had chosen the end of war as their topic. And he joked to the class that the minus was because I'd turned in almost six hundred words and obviously couldn't count.

Years later, I found a book by A. A. Milne called *Peace with Honour*, where he wrote, "It is because I want everybody to think (as I do) that war is poison, and not (as so many think) an over-strong, extremely unpleasant medicine, that I am writing this book."

Christmas furlough that December and January provided the favorite break of my cadetship thus far, and I'm sure it had mostly to do with the new chunk of gold on my finger. However, I chose to wear it only when I knew I wouldn't be around Alf because he wouldn't earn his Citadel ring until the fall of his senior year.

Back at VMI, I had given some serious thought to asking Virginia if she wanted to come down to TR after Christmas. However, I decided against it. In retrospect, it likely had more to do with Carolina than I cared to admit.

Right before heading home, I received the first of many notes from Nick Adams. It said he'd really enjoyed spending time with me and that he hoped to see me a lot more during my cadetship and after graduation. Nick, who I'd already grown to love like a father in some ways, also enclosed a copy of a magazine article he'd written, saying he thought I should learn more about the area where I was attending college because it held a special place in his heart.

It was called "Come See Virginia's Shenandoah Valley" and included a line from the song "Shenandoah," which the VMI band often played at parades, and which typically brings tears to my eyes whether I hear it in the Valley or further afield. In that article, Nick introduced me to places I'd grow to love, including the panhandle area of West Virginia, the pretty town of Winchester, Skyline Caverns and other underground caverns in the Valley, Strasburg, Route 11 Potato Chips, Staunton, Natural Bridge, and Roanoke. Of course, I already knew a bit about lovely Lexington, but I learned a lot more from the article and in coming years.

ALF

———■———

I'LL ALWAYS REMEMBER an assignment I had in my English lit class after we got back from Thanksgiving break. I really enjoyed the class and all of the assigned reading, as well as the unique essay topics the professor gave us. For the last essay assignment of the semester that December, she asked us to write no more than a thousand words about the end of anything, saying any topic was fair game. Recalling a football game back in November where one of our linemen was carted off the field on a stretcher, I chose to write about the end of football far in the future.

THE END OF FOOTBALL
by Alf Marshall

As with many good things that happen in this world, it all began with someone's mom. She was one of those mothers who always made her son wear a helmet when he biked, even if it was just around the corner to his best friend's house. She was one of those mothers who wouldn't let her son play Pop Warner football, and she never gave in to the begging from the son—or the father.

The boy's father had played running back in a Pop Warner league back in the late 1990s but was never any good. Still, he thought the camaraderie of team sports might be good for his small, quiet son. The father and son didn't succeed in convincing the wife and mother until their little boy grew into a bulky and gregarious teenager. So, at fourteen, the boy finally tried out for his school's team.

Of course, he made the team and the head coach made him a starting fullback on the first day of practice with helmets and pads. That 2018 team and the one the following year went undefeated, and the boy was always the one given the ball when it was third or fourth and short and they just needed him to head-rush his way into the defensive line of invariably smaller boys.

The mother never went to a single game, and the boy and the father never talked about the brutality of some of the tackles, even considering the age and size of most of his opponents. The mother did, however, bleach, wash, and fold his grass- and dirt-stained white uniform after every one of those games. There was blood on his uniform more times than she cared to count.

The son's continuing growth and success on the field led to talk of a football scholarship to State even before his junior year in 2020. Again, the team went undefeated. Again, the mother never came to a game.

Their first home game his senior year was on September 11, 2021. A memorial service honoring those who had died twenty years earlier was planned prior to kickoff, and the boy's patriotic mother said she would attend the ceremony and then head home.

After the somber ceremony, the mother stopped to speak with a friend and did not even notice the kickoff and first offensive plays that were taking place behind her. She was halfway to the exit when she heard a sound she'd never forget. It was like two plastic spoons being harmlessly banged together but amplified a hundredfold in the crisp and clear September air, allowing the sound to be carried swiftly to her and echo in her brain the rest of her life.

On the third play of the game, her son had been called upon to gain two yards for a first down, something he'd done dozens of times. This time, however, one of his team's new tackles had missed a blocking assignment, and the surprised defensive lineman found himself lowering his head and helmet to tackle the offense's equally surprised star fullback. The clash of helmets echoed off the concrete of the large home bleachers, the small set of aluminum bleachers on the visitors' side, and even the brick high school's façade in the distance.

Silence filled the stadium as the coaches ran onto the field and both teams backed away from the boy, crumpled on the thirty-yard line. The mother ran back toward the field but was stopped by her husband on the sidelines before they walked hand in hand toward their boy. An ambulance parked nearby was on the field quickly, and the eerily still boy was gently lifted into the flashing vehicle of life—and death.

But the boy didn't die. However, some said the life he led was like a death on earth. He was paralyzed just below his fractured neck and would spend the rest of his days at home with his parents. His helmet stayed on his closet shelf. His never-washed uniform was on the floor in a box.

Yes, by 2021, football helmets were much improved and head injuries were at their lowest number in history. But all of the statistics didn't matter to the mother, or the boy and his father.

Only one statistical number mattered to the mother every time she woke up and helped her son get into his wheelchair. And that number was zero. She wanted zero football injuries from head to toe, and she knew the only way that would happen would be the end of football.

She used all of the social media avenues available at the time to get the support of one mother at a time. She decided if they could end football at the youngest level, they could eventually end football at the high school, college, and professional levels. And she was right, one mother at a time.

It took her—and eventually tens of thousands of other mothers across America—fifteen long years for the final football game to take place in the United States. Ironically, it was the NFL championship game in January of 2036. It could no longer even go by its former superfluous name because the league had dwindled to just eight teams by then, and it was televised only on the internet, to be watched by the sport's few remaining fans.

The mother left it to others to research how many concussions and other injuries would be avoided every year for eternity. Her final social media post, which she wrote with her son staring at the screen with her, said, "The end of football. January 30, 2036."

I remember the professor gave me the only A I received in that class for the essay. I also recall being glad that we didn't have football players in that class to give me grief about my topic.

My junior year's Christmas furlough back home was generally like the previous two midwinter breaks, except learning about Ben's end-of-war essay, of course, and its similarity to mine. I also thought more often about being closer to graduation and the Marine Corps. I was still quite stoic about my experiences at The Citadel, but my family and Carolina seemed to be honoring their own sort of "Don't ask, don't tell" policy. Which had nothing to do with the military policies about gays at the time.

CAROLINA

———○———

DURING ONE OF our school breaks junior year, Ben asked Alf if he was looking forward to getting his class ring the following fall, and he said he was, but his answer didn't seem to match the enthusiasm I'd heard from other Citadel cadets and alums. When Alf left the kitchen to go to the bathroom a few minutes later, Ben caught my eye, held up his ringless right hand, and quietly said, "That's exactly why I'm not wearing my ring, Carolina."

That sentiment quickly shifted during Alf's fourth and final year at The Citadel, when he was focused on getting his class ring and then the march to graduation. The ring came first, on a warm fall day that was filled with anticipation. And a surprise.

After the formal ring ceremony in McAlister Field House, Alf found me and his mom outside on the sidewalk, and he had a bigger smile than I'd seen since he left for school. I gave him a long hug, and after I finally pulled away, he turned to embrace his mother.

"I'm proud of you, Alf," Marge said, holding him at arm's length.

"Me too," I added, looking down at a small box he was carrying that I assumed held his ring.

But Alf turned to me, held up the box in his ring-clad left hand, and said, "This is for you, Car. You deserve it as much as me or any of my classmates—or their girlfriends or fiancées, for that matter."

I knew immediately what the blue velvet Jostens box held. I opened it to find a miniature version of his Citadel class ring. His mom exclaimed, "Oh, Carolina. And, oh, Alf," as he slipped it out of the box and slid it on my right ring finger.

Of course, it was a perfect fit. "How did you know my size?" I asked, holding it up for the two of them to admire.

"Oh, that was easy. My mom called your mom, and she looked it up on the receipt she had for the UNC ring you ordered. Well, do you like it, Car?"

"I love it, Alf. I'll treasure it forever. Thank you so much for thinking of me on what's supposed to be your special day and weekend."

"This just made it even more special, didn't it, Mom?"

"I knew it would, you two," she said, still grinning ear to ear. She hugged me again, saying, "I could barely keep from telling you when I picked you up in Chapel Hill yesterday. I could already picture it on your finger, just like Alf's. And Ben's too, actually."

"I wish Ben could have been here," said Alf. "But he'd already be bragging to anyone who would listen how much bigger his VMI ring is than mine. And how they get their rings a year earlier than us. Of course, it might just get him slugged in this town." Alf smirked at the thought.

Marge and I tried to keep the focus on Alf for the rest of the weekend, and it was easy to do thanks to his classmates receiving most of the attention as well. But I couldn't help occasionally glancing down at my new ring and smiling. And whenever I did, I'd look up and see Alf gazing at me with what I knew was satisfaction and pride. When Marge was with us, I could see the same thoughts in her smiling eyes.

With that ring, it was like Alf made me a classmate in a class of just two. With that ring, Alf bonded me to him—and The Citadel— forever. I wore that ring every day starting that afternoon, until circumstances none of us could have predicted led me to remove it.

ALF

OF COURSE, PUTTING my Citadel ring on for the first time was a landmark event of my four years in Charleston. But I found myself just as excited to place the miniature on Carolina's finger. It may sound trite to say it, but that little ring was a thank-you for what she'd endured because of what I was enduring—and a blessing for being beside me in body, and sometimes only in spirit, during what had become a scary new world for anyone serving this country.

As my ring bonded me to my classmates forever, her ring bonded us together. And it also bound Carolina to The Citadel. From that day forward, it seemed that for Carolina The Citadel had become a friend instead of a foe. I'm not exactly sure why, but the rings made it all weirdly worthwhile. They also gave my remaining time at The Citadel even more purpose, as well as renewed determination for what was to follow.

Ben had received his VMI ring the fall before me, and I found myself regretting I hadn't asked him more about what it meant to him. I knew he had taken another cadet he'd befriended to their dance—a Virginian named Virginia, ironically—but, for me, that couldn't compare to what Car and I shared the weekend I gave her the ring.

The rest of the fall went quickly, as many Citadel seniors in earlier classes that I'd gotten to know had predicted. Charleston was as pretty as ever that fall and even into December, and with my lighter academic load and military commitments, I even made two trips home and one to Chapel Hill when there weren't football games or other conflicts. I also had time to explore downtown and the Charleston peninsula more than I had been able to my first three years at The Citadel.

BEN

————— ◆ —————

I DIDN'T GO to The Citadel for Alf's ring ceremony, deciding instead to head to Richmond with Virginia, and didn't think twice about it until my mom told me by phone on Sunday that my brother had given Carolina a miniature version of his Citadel ring. I'll always regret not being there to see him give it to her, but I still love hearing Mom and Car repeat the story today.

I'd never thought of my brother as being romantic, but I think that, besides his love of—and service to—our country, his choice to give Car that ring was surely one of the most loving things he'd do in his life. Like his Citadel ring and my VMI ring, that now-worn miniature serves as a physical reminder to Carolina of Alf, The Citadel, the Marine Corps, and so much more.

I look back on that fall in Lexington and my time in Richmond with Virginia's extended family as being among the best periods I enjoyed while a cadet. I had more free time on post and in town, several free weekends to go to Richmond, and even got back to Travelers Rest occasionally to share time with my mom, and sometimes Carolina and her parents, as well as Alf on the rare occasion he'd return home.

I really didn't know Richmond very well until that fall of 2003. I stayed in the big Shields house on Monument Avenue, where Virginia had grown up with her mom and grandparents, Win and Sarah Shields. Virginia later told me that her grandparents specifically requested that I stay in her dad's childhood bedroom.

On those first visits to Richmond, I fell in love with the historic city, and especially the Fan District. Virginia and others, including her mom, her grandparents, and even Nick when he was in town, took great pride in showing me "their" Richmond, and that was especially true when it came to restaurants. Looking back, it was through Fan restaurants that my love of Richmond, and the Shields family of food lovers, deepened.

I've tried to remember all of the restaurants we hit during those weekends away from VMI, including many that are now closed, but I'm pretty sure we went to Davis & Main, John & Norman's, Stonewall Café, Robin Inn, Athens Tavern, and—more than likely—beloved Joe's Inn, where I'm still a regular all these years later. Virginia says she remembers I was the first person she'd seen eat an entire plate of spaghetti à la Joe, with Nick being the second when we returned there with him on a Sunday evening two weeks later.

I'm not sure why I never asked Virginia about going home to TR with me one weekend. In retrospect, I guess it had something to do with the dynamics of being back there with either Alf or Carolina—or maybe even both of them. More than four years after Carolina made her decision, I still felt uncomfortable around them much of the time. And I must have felt—without realizing my reasoning—that having Virginia there would add to those awkward feelings.

CAROLINA

———•————o————•———

CHRISTMAS BREAK OUR senior year was the best any of us could remember during college, and that was mainly due to Alf being in a better emotional state than he'd been in three years. Both Alf and Ben wore their rings proudly, and I realized that Ben had not worn his VMI ring during the last twelve months when we were all back in TR.

Christmas seemed better when it came to our interactions, too. I think it was still the most awkward for Ben, who likely felt he'd been the third wheel for years. And now I wore a Citadel ring. I know that Alf tried his best to include Ben more often, and I did love their initial banter about the size of their respective rings, but there remained the ring of truth that I had chosen Alf over Ben—and that I wore a Citadel miniature and not one from VMI.

The return to our schools in mid-January for our final semesters and graduations would write three closing chapters for three very different college careers. It also led to the start of a Marine Corps career for Alf and my "career" as a military spouse, though I had plans to continue some sort of work in journalism. But I had no idea what form that would take—or where it would take place.

I continued to regularly write about sorority life for *The Daily Tar Heel*, and I also received several other writing assignments about campus life, events, and more. One of the stories was about Charles Kuralt and his UNC legacy. I also continued volunteering at the Charles Kuralt Center, which drew me even closer to the man, his words, and that powerful baritone voice that brought his stories from the road to life.

Graduation came much too quickly, but I knew it was time to move on. Of course, the pomp and circumstance of my graduation paled in comparison to Alf's at The Citadel—or Ben's commencement ceremony in Lexington, from what I heard from his mom. I was glad their mom could attend both graduations, as well as share what I thought would be my last day in Chapel Hill with me.

BEN

◆

WE HAD THE final parade of our cadetships on a sunny Friday afternoon, and Letcher Avenue was as packed as I ever saw it for a parade. The Class of 2004, our class, marched in formation, and the band played "Shenandoah," still as poignant now as then.

We marched through Jackson Arch, where I couldn't resist looking up at that Jackson quote one final time. *"You may be whatever you resolve to be."* How many other VMI boys becoming men, and girls becoming women, had stared at that quote and questioned their resolve to become a VMI graduate? I certainly had at times, but I'd made it, and so had all of my classmates, including Virginia.

Someone then opened the courtyard's lone fire hydrant, and a corner of the courtyard was quickly flooded and muddy. Our well-liked First Class president, who was commissioning in the Marine Corps and would lose his life in Afghanistan, was the first to take a running start and do a belly flop into the mud, sliding a good ten feet before coming to a sloppy halt near the first stoop's rusty railings. I've always wondered how this tradition started, and I'm assuming, like many things at VMI, it was long ago.

When he jumped up with hands held above his head, his face was covered in mud, and you could only see the whites of his eyes and teeth as the Second Class banged their rings on the railings up on second stoop, the Thirds jealously watched, and the Fourths gave their dykes and the Class of 2004 a final old yell.

A dozen or so of my classmates went next, and that corner of the courtyard quickly became filled with Firsts in and around the mud. Of course, Virginia was among the first to go, nailing her belly flop and long slide, and then rolling around in the mud with everyone else. I followed in the next wave and found her for a muddy hug that we both let linger as long as seemed appropriate. And, yes, we locked eyes after we hugged.

Saturday morning was crystal clear, and it would have been a perfect day for graduation on the Parade Ground as they once did, weather permitting, until the early-1980s. Now, though, graduation was held in Cameron Hall, our basketball facility that could really rock during certain games, including whenever The Citadel roundball team came to town. Nick had told me that Cameron Hall opened when he was a cadet, after decades of playing games in "the Pit," where boisterous cadets had been famous for intimidating visiting players, coaches, and even referees.

In a typical example of VMI alumni success and loyalty, Cameron Hall was almost completely funded by the Cameron brothers of Wilmington, North Carolina—1938 and 1942 graduates. The sparkling baseball diamond was also funded by two other VMI grads from Richmond, and I still get back to that gem of a ballpark for several games a year.

Cameron Hall didn't provide the same graduation atmosphere as the Parade Ground, but none of us really cared as we walked across the stage to receive our diplomas.

In some ways, that singular moment went way too quickly. I was certainly glad when my name was called and I took my diploma from the dean before shaking hands with the superintendent and saying thanks. But I had to grab the railing on the way down the steps because my legs were so shaky. I can still picture the moment we threw our white gloves into the air to signify the end of graduation and the beginning of our post-VMI lives.

ALF

——■——

ALTHOUGH EARNING RECOGNITION as a class back in the spring of 2001 after our trying Knob experience and receiving my coveted Citadel ring the previous semester were highlights of college life in Charleston, my final semester at The Citadel remains my favorite time as a cadet.

Of course, I had more freedom and free hours than any other time of my cadetship, allowing me to head home to Travelers Rest once and Chapel Hill twice, as well as my first and only visit to Lexington to see Ben and his VMI. The similarities between the two schools and the experiences for the cadets were not lost on me, and I found myself wishing I'd spent more time talking to Ben about our shared military school experiences the past four years.

May graduations for the three of us arrived all too quickly. My mother and Carolina were able to attend my graduation, and my mom even went to Chapel Hill with Carolina's parents for her graduation as well when I couldn't go due to a Marine Corps ROTC obligation. Mom also headed to Lexington for Ben's graduation, which she said was remarkably similar to The Citadel's ceremony two days earlier.

The two things I recall about my graduation were two of the speeches. The commencement speaker was none other than Mayor Joe Riley, who was a 1964 Citadel grad and a great orator like Pat Conroy.

Following a long Citadel tradition, the "last" graduate was also allowed to make brief remarks. I can't remember his name, but I'm pretty sure it started with a *Z*, and his brief speech involved the recounting of some of the funnier times during his, and our, cadetships.

I was commissioned as a Marine Corps second lieutenant the day before graduation. Ironically, the ROTC advisor I'd twice bared my soul to commissioned me. Thus began the step-off for yet another life-changing march, not knowing where those steps would lead me—or Carolina.

CAROLINA

—————○—————

JUST A FEW days after we graduated, Alf and I were married.

We chose Clearview Baptist Church, which we'd both attended on and off as kids, but—as often happened—had stopped going most Sundays once we hit our mid-teens. Neither my parents or Marge asked or pressured any of us to continue attending once we started high school. But the old church still held a special place in my heart as a place of peace.

Although many recent grads chose The Citadel's Summerall Chapel for their wedding, we decided against it. Alf did ask if he could wear his Marine Corps dress blues uniform for the first time, and of course I said yes, even though that uniform didn't signify peace to me.

When I look back at our wedding pictures from that day, Alf looks so handsome and happy. He'd earned that uniform—and the honor to wear it on one of the most important days of our life together.

We'd planned on a simple wedding, with fewer than fifty people invited to the service and reception. I opted for just one bridesmaid in Lisa Dunn, my roommate and best friend back in Chapel Hill. One of Alf's roommates his last two years at The Citadel, who wore his new dress blues uniform from the Army, was his lone usher. My father gave me away, and, of course, Ben was Alf's best man.

The day before the wedding, we met with Kevin Caudill, the minister at Clearview, to discuss our vows, deciding on the traditional wording he suggested for both of us. However, on the walk back to my house, hand in hand, Alf was quiet.

"A penny for your thoughts?" I asked, stopping him at the brick walk leading up to our front porch.

He turned to me and paused before responding with a question of his own. "What do you think about us not using that 'til death do us part' part?"

I returned the gaze I'd grown to love, thought about it for a few seconds, and said, "Of course, Alf. I'd love that." I squeezed his hand, held his eyes, and tried to lighten the mood by smiling and asking, "Do you know something I don't?"

He laughed and pulled me up the walk toward our house, but I knew I'd struck a chord. As a soon-to-be Marine Corps wife, I already knew that death and service are inevitably intertwined in real life. And, of course, since 9/11, I knew that Alf also understood this all too well.

So, on a sunny and blue-sky Saturday, we exchanged vows before the small group of friends and family we'd invited to share the day with us, with the minister quickly finishing the rest of the service in what now seems like a blur from another life.

We had the reception in downtown Greenville in the upstairs part of Soby's, which they'd been nice enough to let us rent on a busy Saturday evening.

My mom, Marge, Alf, and I had decided to keep the food as simple as the ceremony, with passed hors d'oeuvres and just two entrée options.

Everyone had a choice of filet mignon or crab cakes for their entrée, with both Alf and me opting for the crab cakes as a sort of homage to The Citadel, Charleston, and Chef Frank Lee at Slightly North of Broad. I smiled when I noticed that almost everyone from the Upcountry, except Ben and Marge, and anywhere else inland opted for the filet, while those from the Lowcountry and other coastal areas went for the crab cakes.

I couldn't stop thinking about Alf leaving the next day for Quantico, while I stayed back home in TR, so there's little I remember about that night. I do recall dancing with Ben to a funky, little-known song from Hootie & the Blowfish called "Little Brother." Alf had latched onto the song when the album came out, and he occasionally called Ben by the moniker, which his twin brother had earned by being born mere minutes after Alf came screaming headlong into the world. Or so I'm told.

As planned with my mom, I danced with my dad to Celine Dion's "Because You Loved Me." My slow dance with Alf was to what we had deemed "our song" back in college: "I'll Be," a ballad from Greenville native Edwin McCain that had become very popular at weddings.

My mother came to get us at ten o'clock sharp to make our grand exit while most of our guests were still there. I hugged my mother and father, as well as my new mother-in-law, and Alf and I took the short walk across Main Street to the grand old Poinsett Hotel and our march toward another life.

BEN

◆

THOUGH MANY PEOPLE assumed it was required, you didn't have to go into the military post-VMI. After graduation, as planned, I moved to Richmond to start a job as a salesperson with Luck Stone. Growing up in Travelers Rest fueled my love of the outdoors, which gave me an appreciation for natural things. I love the feel and look of stone that came from the earth, and still do. Luck Stone was founded by a VMI grad and had a reputation for hiring VMI alumni. I thought it was the perfect job for me. Of course, the irony of Carolina's maiden name of Stone was not lost on me and many others.

After I helped Virginia store her few civilian belongings at the Shields house up the street from the apartment I'd rented, she went to Military Intelligence Officer Basic Camp at Fort Huachuca out in Arizona, where she said it was hotter than Fort Bragg ever was that summer we went there for training back in 2003. After she returned to Richmond from Fort Huachuca and before reporting to the Pentagon, Virginia casually asked me if she could use my spare bedroom when she was, occasionally, back in Richmond. She said she felt staying at the Shields house up the street gave her grandparents undue worry. Of course, I agreed without hesitation. Once she completed that course and another secretive one that she's never shared with me, she was assigned to the Pentagon, just as she'd always hoped.

From the start of her Army career, Virginia was determined to be at the Pentagon or any other stateside military installation as little as possible. She always said she wanted to have her boots on the ground, and preferably in the hot desert sand. During her first year of service, she often told me that she could get more done in one day in Afghanistan or other hot spots than she could in a week stateside.

That fall, Virginia generally stayed up in DC during the week, working very long hours and getting little sleep. Most Friday nights, she headed back to Richmond, stopping to see her mom and grandparents first and typically getting to my apartment around nine. We'd then share a beer or two and maybe some leftover pizza, if one or both of us hadn't eaten yet.

Often, we stayed up late talking about her work, at least what she could tell me that wasn't classified. We sometimes started a movie, but, inevitably, Virginia was dog-tired from too little sleep during the week, falling sound asleep beside me on the couch.

On one of those Friday nights in late October, I awoke with a start to find Virginia fast asleep with her head in my lap. Looking down at her, I couldn't help but reflect on the life she'd led and was leading. I felt so lucky to be part of the extended Shields family in my own small way, and bent to give her a light kiss on her smooth forehead, just below her blond hairline.

Just as I was drawing away, she slowly opened her eyes and let out a soft sigh. Still holding my gaze, she reached up with her left ring-clad hand and pulled me back to her for our first real kiss.

With one thing inevitably leading to the next, the rest of that memorable night and morning with Virginia changed our relationship. She moved into my room with her few belongings that afternoon, and we were together from that day forward. At least, when she was back in Richmond.

PART V

CAROLINA

———○———

THE SPOUSE OF a Marine leads a unique life, and each of our experiences is different, depending on where our Marine is posted and also when and where he or she is inevitably deployed. The deployments are what we spouses share most, in many ways. We share the loneliness. We share the general ignorance of what's happening. And, most of all, we share the fear.

Like many Marines, Alf's time with the Marine Corps took him several times to sprawling Quantico Marine Corps Base in Virginia and Jacksonville's Camp Lejeune in North Carolina, for varying periods of time. As he was during most of his cadetship, Alf was stoic about his service in general, and his deployments specifically.

I knew that there were some things he couldn't talk about, but I also knew from other Marine Corps wives that there were many things about his work that he could share but didn't. I was aware that he knew of the gruesome deaths of several enlisted soldiers and officers he'd trained with or otherwise knew. I never had the heart to ask him about that, or if he'd ever had to kill anyone.

Just like 9/11 back in Chapel Hill, I'll always remember where I was when I learned Alf was dead. Unlike the tragedies in 2001, which occurred on a Tuesday, it was a Sunday. As I often did on Sunday mornings in TR, I went over to have a cup of coffee with Marge.

I hadn't known Ben was home, but I was glad to learn he was in town when I saw his old brown BMW in their driveway. I was even happier when I walked into their kitchen and saw that Virginia had come with him from Richmond. They were all sitting at the kitchen table.

After hugs all around, we sat back down at the worn table with a glass carafe of coffee from Marge's well-used Mr. Coffee machine on the counter. It was just like so many times before, many years ago, but with Virginia sitting where Alf had sat. While water and milk had been the beverages of choice during those earlier times together, it now was more likely to be iced or hot coffee or tea, or the occasional beer for the boys and wine for Marge and me.

For a half hour or so, I played catch-up with Ben and Virginia about their life in Richmond and caught them up on my month in TR after Alf deployed to Iraq. Then, we heard a loud knock on the door.

Without thinking that anyone would typically have used the doorbell instead of knocking, I remember I thought that it was probably my father hoping to say hello to Ben when he'd seen his car in the driveway. I had the fleeting thought, though, that my father would have come to the back door.

Marge went to the door, and the three of us sat silently looking into our cups. We heard a male voice, but not what was being said. The next sounds I heard were the heart-wrenching wails from Marge and the sound of Ben's chair falling over backwards as he jumped to his feet and rushed out of the kitchen to the front door. Virginia took my hand and held on tight as I realized that the world as I'd known it was crumbling around me and would never be the same after that terrible July day.

Marge and Ben brought the two messengers of death into the kitchen. One, who I later learned was a Marine major, told me that we lost Alf in a battle in Ramadi, Iraq. I never saw the faces of the two men who had the somber duty of telling me my husband had died on the field of honor, which is a phrase I hate to this day. I simply continued to stare into my coffee cup.

I couldn't tell you a single word that was said around that kitchen table after they'd left. I can only tell you that Virginia never let go of my hand.

Alf was buried with full military honors in Travelers Rest at Mountain View Memorial Park, beside his father and in the shadow of his beloved Paris Mountain. After the short church service in Furman's Daniel Chapel, which was arranged by my dad and conducted by the pastor who'd married us, I stood near the foot of the coffin at Mountain View, between Marge and Ben, holding their hands, with Virginia at Ben's side. A uniformed chaplain, who I later learned was a 1967 Citadel grad and a classmate of Pat Conroy's at The Citadel, recited the cadet prayer from memory. He never let his eyes leave mine.

> Almighty God, the source of light and strength, we implore Thy blessing on this our beloved institution, that it may continue true to its high purposes.
>
> Guide and strengthen those upon whom rests the authority of government; enlighten with wisdom those who teach and those who learn; and grant to all of us that through sound learning and firm leadership, we may prove ourselves worthy citizens of our country, devoted to truth, given to unselfish service, loyal to every obligation of life and above all to Thee.
>
> Preserve us faithful to the ideals of The Citadel, sincere in fellowship, unswerving in duty, finding joy in purity, and confidence through a steadfast faith.
>
> Grant to each one of us, in his own life, a humble heart, a steadfast purpose, and a joyful hope, with a readiness to endure hardship and suffer if need be, that truth may prevail among us and that Thy will may be done on earth.
>
> Through Jesus Christ, Our Lord. Amen.

They then played "Taps," the bugler slowly sounding the somber notes. I saw Ben mouth the words to it, realizing for the first time that "Taps" had words:

Day is done, gone the sun,
From the lake, from the hills, from the sky;
All is well, safely rest, God is nigh.

Fading light, dims the sight,
And a star gems the sky, gleaming bright.
From afar, drawing nigh, falls the night.

Thanks and praise, for our days,
Neath the sun, neath the stars, neath the sky;
As we go, this we know, God is nigh.

Sun has set, shadows come,
Time has fled, Scouts must go to their beds
Always true to the promise that they made.

While the light fades from sight,
And the stars gleaming rays softly send,
To thy hands we our souls, Lord, commend.

As the last note was sounded, Ben put my hand in Virginia's and slowly walked to Alf's burnished coffin. He stopped at the head of the coffin and looked straight at me, placing his ring-clad right hand on the coffin and, in a whir, before I saw it coming, brought it down with a loud bang. It was like a gunshot in the still air.

Everyone was jumpy, including me, of course. In the years since 9/11, we all still had thoughts about guns and terrorists. But it's what came next that I'll always remember most about that day.

Without a word, more than a dozen men and women, most of whom were in uniforms from the Marines, the Army, the Air Force, The Citadel, and even VMI, stepped forward in a solemn parade that soon surrounded the coffin completely. One of the Marines, a man named Rob Morley who had made a point to search me out before the service, held my gaze along with Ben.

Virginia was one of those who had gone to stand by Alf as well, after placing my hand in Marge's before following Ben and the others to the coffin. And, once again, Ben raised his hand, followed by other hands gleaming with bands of gold, and began a resounding salute of rings, which seemed to echo off Paris Mountain and all the way to Charleston, Lexington, and even Iraq.

Ben then raised his hand from the coffin and again looked to me and Marge in turn, before simply saying, "Semper fi, brother," while saluting, with the others following suit with somber salutes as well.

BEN

———◆———

LIKE ALMOST EVERYONE in the world—except Virginia and maybe half the population of Iraq, at most—I'd never heard of the city of Ramadi until I read a short article about some fighting there. I didn't even know if Alf was anywhere near the city, though I did know his boots were most definitely on the ground somewhere in Iraq, after Carolina had mentioned it in passing. She didn't like to talk about the details of Alf's Iraq deployment, and I respected and understood that completely.

After Alf graduated from The Citadel, and his marriage to Carolina, he'd headed to The Basic School, which I'd learned to call "TBS" from Marine Corps ROTC brother Rats back at VMI. This took place at the fabled Marine Corps Base Quantico, on the Potomac River. Alf and Carolina had jointly decided that she would not accompany him to Quantico; junior officers who brought their wives for TBS and most other training were generally looked down upon by their fellow Marines.

I remember Carolina telling me by phone from TR that Alf had said it was "hotter than Hades" when he reported to Quantico in mid-June, graduating from TBS six long—for him, I assume— months later. After Carolina had visited Alf at Quantico over Thanksgiving, his graduation timing allowed him to head home for a short Christmas stay. After spending Christmas morning with the Shields family, Virginia and I headed to TR for a few days.

Alf told me when I saw him that a brother Rat of mine had been in his TBS class and that he was really impressed by what VMI had produced, me notwithstanding, he jokingly added. He also told me that the humidity of Quantico in June had switched to icy mornings by December, but that they still kept training to kill in that Virginia soil.

Of course, I didn't know that was the last time I'd see my brother. I still haven't found the strength to reach out to the BR Alf mentioned.

Alf next headed back to Quantico for the Infantry Officer Course, known as IOC in the Corps. He told me in February on a quick phone call, which included Virginia on the other line, that it was the most brutal two months of training he'd experienced. That was saying something, coming from Alf.

From there, my brother received permanent change of station orders, or PCS, for sprawling and sandy Camp Lejeune on the coast of North Carolina. Finally, after his initial eight months on active duty, Carolina was able to join him. She told me later that they had a cute little cottage on post, and I now wish I'd visited them while Alf was stationed there, before his deployment.

After Alf died, I contacted a VMI grad who was stationed at Camp Lejeune, and he helped me get permission to visit the base and see it through Alf's eyes. I'm pretty confident, based on Carolina's description, that I found their house, though I never told her or my mom about my visit.

I started researching the history of Camp Lejeune and learned that it was named for General John A. Lejeune, a Naval Academy grad, thirteenth commandant of the Marine Corps, and the commanding general of the 2nd Army Division in the First World War. I knew Lejeune's name because VMI's Lejeune Hall, which was torn down in 2006 to make room for Third Barracks, was also named for the decorated veteran, who, after he retired from the Marine Corps, also served from 1929 to 1937 as the Institute's fifth superintendent.

I remembered Alf telling me that he'd heard a Marine Corps veteran named Patrick Brent speak about Lejeune, who pronounced his name with an *r* in it, like "Luh-journ." Brent said that pronunciation was historically correct and the way family members still pronounced it. Most everyone at VMI pronounced it "Luh-june," except for cadets enrolled in Naval and Marine ROTC or Marine or Naval officers and enlisted members posted there.

Brent served with the 4th Marine Division and would go on to become an embedded reporter with the Marines in Iraq and Kuwait, writing for UPI and *Leatherneck*, the national magazine of the Marine Corps, with Marine Corps Lieutenant General Chip Gregson calling Brent "our very own Ernie Pyle" at the sixtieth anniversary of the Battle of Iwo Jima in 2005. Brent obviously had an affinity for the sea and military service and history: other tidbits about him that I learned online included his successful turnaround of Windjammer Cruises in Hawaii, his book of sea stories, *29*, which was published under the pseudonym Tim Monaghan, and his role in the creation and early operation of the Pearl Harbor Visitor Center.

Once he'd completed the required training in Quantico in the spring of 2005, Alf was assigned to Camp Lejeune's thousand-strong 3rd Battalion, 8th Marines. The 3rd was part of the 8th Marine Regiment and in the 2nd Marine Division.

From its founding in San Diego in 1940, Alf's infantry battalion had a long history of conflict and combat, including several World War II battles, like Guadalcanal and Tarawa, the Cuban Missile Crisis, several Marine Amphibious Unit (MAU) missions, including then Major Oliver North in the Mediterranean in 1979, Lebanon, Bosnia, and, of course, Global War on Terror hot spots like Afghanistan, Iraq, and beyond. I later learned that another 8th Marines battalion, the fabled 1st, was nicknamed "the Beirut Battalion" because of the 1983 Beirut barracks bombing when 241 Marines, sailors, and soldiers were lost.

Alf served as a second lieutenant platoon commander of about forty Marines, many of whom had graduated from the tough training at Marine Corps Recruit Depot on South Carolina's Parris Island in

Beaufort the previous year while Alf was in Quantico, as well as a couple of NCOs by way of Marine Corps Recruit Depot, San Diego. I never talked to my brother about the first Marines under his command, though I've since learned that he lost two of them in Ramadi before he himself was killed later that day. I may someday find the strength to contact their families, but it's not likely anytime soon.

In all of my research about Camp Lejeune, I did not try to learn more about the brutal days and months in Ramadi leading up to Alf's death, beyond a few accounts online that never specifically mentioned Alf. I did find one brief account about a specific battle involving something called "Operation Post Virginia," which I found pitifully ironic. Virginia must know about it as well, but she never mentioned it to me, Carolina, or my mom.

Several classmates from VMI who have had to deliver the news to family members have told me that many of them wanted details that were sometimes very difficult for them to share, but why would I want to relive his day of death?

Everything remains a blur about the day we learned of Alf's death and the funeral that followed three days later. I was most amazed by the strength of my mom, Virginia, and even sweet Carolina. I've never asked her, but I wondered if Carolina had somehow been preparing for this time since Alf told us he'd accepted a Navy scholarship with a Marine Corps option.

Alf's brief funeral was at Furman's Daniel Chapel, with a memorial service in the church and the burial service, with full military honors, held graveside at Mountain View Memorial Park, less than five miles north of Furman. Both services were performed, or however you phrase it, by the pastor who'd also married Carolina and Alf.

At Alf's funeral, my mother stood to Carolina's right and I was on her left, with Virginia next to me. There were dozens of other people who had been part of our lives in TR, as well classmates and other alumni from The Citadel and several enlisted Marines and officers from his much-too-short service to his country. The major who'd delivered the news to us stood discreetly behind everyone but was always on alert to help in any way he could.

There were also at least five Citadel cadets in coatees, as well as many other men and women in dress uniform from all four branches. I recognized at least two of them as Citadel classmates of Alf.

I'd been asked to be a pallbearer, but I'd said no. Carrying Alf's casket would have brought me to my knees.

As the last note of "Taps" sounded, I put Carolina's hand in Virginia's and slowly walked over to Alf's burnished coffin, which the funeral home had told Marge was hand-hewn wood harvested from a forest near Travelers Rest; that seemed fitting.

I stopped at the head of the coffin and then looked straight at Carolina before placing my right hand on the coffin and bringing it down with all the force I could muster through my grief and anger.

Though I hadn't thought or planned what would happen after my ringing salute to my brother, more than a dozen men and women in various uniforms came forward to join me. One of the Marines, a chiseled man named Rob Morley, had searched me out before the service, telling me what a great cadet, Marine, and man Alf had been. He had held my hand and gaze until I had to look away. Of course, Virginia had made her way to the coffin as well, placing Carolina's hand in my mom's before coming to us.

Once everyone had joined me at the coffin, I again raised my hand, followed by the others, and began a resounding salute of rings. After a half dozen or more shots into the stillness, I stepped back from the coffin and saluted my brother, saying, "Semper fi, brother." All the others joined me in saluting a fallen brother-in-arms.

After Alf's funeral, Virginia and I returned to Richmond and our new life together, when she was home and not in places like Iraq and Afghanistan. My work at Luck Stone and personal commitments kept me from thinking about Alf every waking hour, as I digested life without him. I thought a lot about Carolina as well, of course. Back in those dark days, I even found myself wondering if I now had a life without Carolina as well, due to our loss of Alf.

I didn't talk to Carolina about her future in TR without Alf. I guess I assumed she would stay in TR, and my mom told me that was her plan. She'd rented a short-term apartment after Alf had been deployed, and I figured she'd probably either extend that or maybe even move back in with her parents.

In the following months, I kept up with Carolina as best I could through my mom, but she said Car had only stopped by the house twice and that, for the first time, their conversations had been awkward. "I think she's still really struggling with being alone for the first time in her life," my mom told me, perhaps two months after the funeral.

When Virginia wasn't in some far-flung corner of the world fighting terrorists known and unknown, she was in Richmond with me on most weekends, commuting to and from the Pentagon Mondays and Fridays. Much of this depended on her workload and the time zones in the places terrorists and American military intelligence types tended to hang out. Our relationship deepened, and I think everyone, including Virginia and me, believed we would get married at some point. Gin and I hadn't talked about it, and I guess Alf's death and her constant time overseas in harm's way delayed the discussion and decision.

CAROLINA

———○———

LIFE MARCHES ON, as it must. After Alf's death, I made the decision with my parents and Marge to stay in Travelers Rest and continue my pursuit of a career in freelance journalism. Alf's life insurance policy with the Marine Corps, plus a monthly payment awkwardly called "Dependency and Indemnity Compensation," allowed much flexibility in my new life alone. Of course, no amount of compensation would bring Alf back to me.

About a week after the funeral, and with Alf-like determination, I finally stopped wandering around the apartment and holding things Alf had touched before his deployment. During that first terrible week, I'd even slept with some of his things, including a uniform top he'd left behind when he went to Iraq. It still held a hint of his scent, and for the first few nights after the funeral, I fell asleep to that smell.

But I washed that uniform top exactly seven days after the service, and I marched through our little apartment, quickly deciding to part with many things small and large that I knew would remind me of times and places to which I could never see myself returning. Some things, like Alf's Citadel diploma and his Citadel ring, I put aside for Marge and Ben, respectively. I put many items in a closet in the guest bedroom so I wouldn't see them every day, including the miniature Citadel ring Alf had given me back in May 2004. I somehow found the strength to donate Alf's civilian clothes and some other personal items I simply couldn't keep in the apartment. However, you can't discard memories like you can material things.

One thing I found that will never be discarded was a letter inside the Bible Alf kept in his bedside table.

My Dearest Carolina,

If you are reading this letter, I'm no longer with you in the physical sense. But know that I'll still always be with you in my heart and soul and that we will be reunited someday in whatever heaven our God has created for those we love. Death will not part us.

As I write this, I can't know what Ben's situation will be, but know that I have asked him to take care of you in every way that you may need. He has promised me with his blood that he will do this for me—and you.

Please know that I've loved every minute of my life with you, through good times and bad, when you were always at my side. Thank you for making the choice you did all those years ago. I love you.

Semper Fi,
Alf

BEN

ABOUT A MONTH after the funeral, I got a call from Rob Morley, the Citadel grad I briefly met at Alf's funeral. He said he was stationed up I-95 at Quantico and told me that he and Alf had reconnected when Alf was in Quantico for The Basic School. Rob then asked if I'd be able to see him if he drove down from Quantico one day. I responded yes to any opportunity to stay connected with my brother.

Rob, with his taut features and sheared scalp, looked like a Marine uncomfortable out of uniform when he came down to Richmond a few days later. He drove south early in the morning to avoid DC traffic in both directions, arriving at my apartment around eight. Virginia was out of the country. After I poured steaming cups of black coffee for both of us, we went out to my small balcony overlooking Monument Avenue.

With the bluntness I'd come to expect of Marines, Rob got right to the heart of the matter before I even knew there was a matter. "You do know your brother was gay, right, Ben?"

I didn't know this, nor had I ever thought it. So of course I said he wasn't.

"There's no way, Rob," I replied, my voice low, staring into my coffee cup and refusing to make eye contact.

"I understand your reaction, Ben. I can tell you that I know he hid it well from everyone." I still couldn't look at him, though I knew he was staring at me. "I should know. I've been doing the same for more than a decade."

At that, my head jerked, and I met his steely stare. "You mean he told you? You mean you were both gay?" I asked, incredulous. "What, were you lovers or something?" I sneered, knowing my voice betrayed my anger . . . and fear.

"No, Ben, we were not lovers. I need to tell you how I know, and my mission here will be accomplished. Please hear me out, and then I will leave you in peace."

"I most certainly will not be in peace after you leave, Rob, but do your business and then leave, please."

"Thank you. Please know I've never told anyone this, and that my decision to tell you has not come easily.

"As I mentioned to you at the funeral, I was a senior when Alf was a Knob back in the fall of 2000, when he reported to The Citadel. I was in the same company and barracks as Alf.

"I guess it was October when it happened. I'd never laid eyes on Alf until that day, as far as I can remember. As you know, male Knobs, and Rats at VMI, I guess, looked so similar back then, with their heads pretty much shaved. Still do, I guess.

"Anyway, I rarely yelled at Knobs during my three years as an upperclassman, but I had just returned from what I knew was a less than stellar performance on a math test and wasn't in a great mood. I'd caught Alf's eye when he passed and had angrily asked him what he was staring at.

"He immediately stopped and, now staring straight ahead, yelled, 'Nothing, sir!' Well, I got in his face, locked eyes with him, and quietly said, 'So, I'm nothing, huh, Knob?'"

"'No sir, you're something, sir,' he responded quietly.

"'That's better, Knob. Why so meek? You gay or something?' It was a question I'd asked a few Knobs over the previous three years. It was my admittedly weird way of staving off thoughts by other cadets that I was a homosexual.

"Your brother still held my stare, but something in his eyes told me that my offhand question had struck a nerve. After another moment's pause, he simply whispered, 'Yes, sir.'

"I realize you can't understand this, and I don't expect you to, but as a gay man, I simply and positively knew he was telling me the truth. You're shaking your head in denial as I say this, Ben, but I knew.

"After what was likely just seconds but felt like long minutes, I said, 'March on, Knob, and hope I never see you again.'

"Of course, Alf couldn't have known that his secret was safe with me. He'd fortunately shared his homosexuality with one of very few cadets who wouldn't have pounced on his quiet admittance. Then and now, I assumed it was due to our honor code and Alf's subsequent fear of telling any sort of lie by saying he wasn't gay.

"If I had it to do again, Ben, and I've often thought of this, I would have found Alf in barracks later that day and told him in private that his secret was safe with me. I don't know for certain why I didn't, though I suspect it was my first experience with someone else, besides myself, I mean, with the 'Don't ask, don't tell' policy prevalent in the military.

"I didn't speak to Alf again during his Knob year, and I learned from him only last year that he spent that long first year in daily fear that I would report him, and he'd possibly have to leave The Citadel in shame.

"In fact, when I ran into Alf at Quantico, he said not only had he spent that year in fear of me ratting him out, but that he remained concerned during his entire cadetship and as a young Marine officer. Until the day we met again.

"He shared this with me over a beer at a place called the Command Post in Q-Town. Only then, years too late, did I tell him that I am, and was, of course, gay as well."

With that, Rob halted his monologue. Finally, after a quiet couple of minutes to reflect on what he'd told me, I looked at him and said, "I guess I have to believe everything you've told me is true, Rob. However, I respectfully request that I'm the only person you ever share this with. Do I have your word?"

He immediately nodded, saying, "Affirmative, Ben. You have my word."

"Well, I guess your work here is done, Rob. I'm sorry for questioning you at first, but I'm sure you of all people understand that this has been a shock. I did not mean to doubt your honor and your intention in any way."

I stood, and Rob got to his feet as well. He put out his ring-clad right hand, saying, "I hope I made the best decision. It's honestly a weight I've carried since that day at The Citadel. I knew I needed to come see you when I heard about Alf's death in Iraq. I actually had several brothers-in-arms who died there during that fighting."

With his hand still in mine, I said, "I understand. Thank you again for coming today. Semper fi, sir," I said, stepping back and saluting him.

"Semper fi, Ben," Rob said, sharply returning my salute.

Of course, I never told Carolina, my mom, or anyone else about Rob Morley and his story. I never will. Ironically, I ran across a picture of Rob many years later when he saw President Obama sign the Don't Ask, Don't Tell Repeal Act of 2010.

CAROLINA

—————○—————

BEN AND, WHEN she could, Virginia returned to TR at least once a month after Alf's funeral. They stayed over at Marge's and were kind enough to include me in everything they did, whether it was a simple supper at the house, meals out in Travelers Rest and Greenville, and even an outing up to Alf's beloved Paris Mountain State Park for a picnic that we put together at the Café at Williams Hardware.

Except for my dad, Ben was practically my only contact with males in the months following Alf's death. I continued to get condolence cards and check-in calls from several of Alf's Citadel classmates and Marine Corps brothers-in-arms, as they referred to themselves, but those cards and calls started to taper off as the lonely months marched forward, though I felt I was at best marching in place.

Several high school friends tentatively asked me about guys who they thought might be interested in asking me on a date, but I always told them no. Alf would always be my guy. Well, I guess Ben and my dad were also my guys in a way and always would be.

My work on *The Daily Tar Heel* had prepared me well for freelance writing, and I kept busy with the local paper, which led to lots of clips and eventual magazine-writing assignments, including my first feature with a national travel magazine called *Trailblazer*.

They paid my expenses in Savannah and Charleston to research the story. It was the first time I'd left Travelers Rest since Alf's death. I needed to move on, literally and figuratively, and I honestly would have completed the assignment for free.

Of course, it was hard to return to Charleston and several of the places that Alf and I had grown to love. However, I definitely saw the city with new eyes, unclouded by Alf's moodiness when he'd been at The Citadel.

It was actually my first visit to Savannah, and a planned three-day trip turned into a week of immersion. I've often returned to the city since then, and my love affair with it grows with each visit.

I was very proud of my love letter to the two cities when *Trailblazer* published it six months after my trips. I was excited to share some Charleston restaurant favorites for me and Alf, like Slightly North of Broad and 82 Queen, as well as new finds like FIG, which I know Alf would have loved. For the Savannah portion of the story, I featured the Olde Pink House after enjoying everything about the dining experience there—except eating alone.

BEN

—————◆—————

YEARS AFTER ALF'S death and funeral, I found myself wondering how his body had made its way from Iraq back to Travelers Rest. I really don't know why, but I called Pete Massie, a classmate from VMI who I knew was still on active duty with the Marine Corps and stationed down in Beaufort on Parris Island.

When I called, the first thing he said was that he heard about Alf the day after it happened, and that he was sorry he was unable to attend the funeral because he was deployed in Afghanistan. "Everyone who knew him said he was a good man and an even better Marine, Ben," he said.

"Thanks, Pete. That means a lot coming from you. Do you have time for a quick question?"

"Sure. Anything, brother Rat. What's on your mind?"

"Well, I was actually there when the news was delivered to Alf's wife and our mom. I can't remember the name of the major who came to the door, but you probably know him. I can't imagine that duty, Pete, you know?"

"I'm afraid I've done it twice already in my short career. It's happening way too often right now."

"Wow. That's gotta be tough."

"It is."

"What I was wondering, Pete, was how Alf's body would have made it back from Iraq. And so quickly."

"Well, I can't actually tell you for sure how it happened in Alf's case, but, sadly, I'm afraid it's become fairly standard procedure. So, it's very likely Alf's body was flown from Iraq to Ramstein Air Base in Germany, then to Delaware's Dover Air Force Base and what they call Mortuary Affairs. There, your brother's body would have been prepared for burial and made to look as presentable as possible in his dress blues, even if no one would ever see his body. And then, finally, to your family in your hometown.

"I want you to know that there's no doubt Alf was treated with utmost respect and dignity every step of the way. It's very likely he always had a Marine at his side or close by. And I can guarantee you that there were a lot, and I mean a lot, of salutes—during the stops on his journey home."

I couldn't help smiling at Pete's Charleston accent. "Well, that certainly gives me some solace, BR. Would it be okay if I passed your report on to Alf's widow and our mom?"

"Of course, Ben. And please tell them both I'd be happy to talk to them, if they ever want to know more."

I was about to say thanks and goodbye when Pete jumped in. "Hey, I just thought of something, and you can take it or you can leave it."

"Fire away, Pete."

"Well, a film came out a few years ago called *Taking Chance*. Kevin Bacon plays a Marine officer who volunteers to accompany the body of a fellow Marine killed in Iraq. It's based on a true story, and I actually served with the officer Bacon portrays in the film. Anyway, you might want to check it out. But I gotta warn you, Ben—it's pretty heart-wrenching. It may hit too close to home, I'm afraid."

"Hmm. Thanks for mentioning it, Pete. I haven't heard of it, but maybe it would provide some more closure, huh?"

"It's possible, yes. I'd definitely watch it before sharing it with Alf's wife or your mom, though. You might be okay with it, but I'm not sure about them."

I found a copy of the DVD on Amazon and ordered it right away but didn't get a chance to watch it for a couple of weeks. I'm sure I was a bit afraid of what I would learn, and I was certainly right about that. I sometimes wish I'd never learned about the film at all.

Like many movies I watched in a big theater or in the living room, I watched it with a bag or bowl of heavily buttered and salted popcorn. I put the DVD in the player and hit play.

Within the first five minutes, I hit pause five times. It took me more than four hours that evening to make my way through the one-hour-and-thirty-minute movie. I took only one bite of the popcorn, finding it distasteful and somehow disrespectful to Alf and the Marine Corps.

I did, however, pour myself two shots of Virginia Gentleman on the rocks. It helped me make my way through the film and my own march through some damn tough memories. I couldn't stomach eating the leftover pizza I had reheated in the microwave.

Pete had warned me it would be difficult to watch, imagining Alf being escorted home to Travelers Rest in a similar manner, and it certainly was. But I was moved and humbled by the respect with which the fallen Marine was treated. I was certain Alf had received the same honor, but that didn't make the film less painful to watch.

As the credits rolled at the end of the film, I decided that I would never share *Taking Chance* with Carolina, my mom, or Virginia. And I haven't.

CAROLINA

OVER THE YEARS, I often wondered about the days following Alf's death, and how his body had made its way back to Travelers Rest. I'd even gone so far as Googling how a Marine killed in action was treated after his death, and how he or she is brought home to "rest in peace," which I always found such a silly phrase and still do.

After glancing at a list of links to military sites that talked about Ramstein Air Base in Germany and something called Dover Port Mortuary in Delaware, I came across a link to a movie. It was called *Taking Chance,* and starred Kevin Bacon, who I'd always loved. I clicked on the link and read a summary of the movie, which said the film was based on a true story, with Bacon playing the role of the officer who brought the Marine home for burial.

Although I briefly thought about ordering the film from Amazon, I decided against it. I also decided not to tell Alf's mom or even Ben or Virginia about the movie. It just hit too close to home, and likely wouldn't make it easier for any of us.

Though I didn't order the film, I did end up reading about something I learned was called, "Bacon's Law," or "Six Degrees of Kevin Bacon." Evidently, there are several versions of it, but the basic premise is that any two people on the planet are just six or less "acquaintance" links apart from the quite prolific actor. The concept evidently originated with the theory that anyone in the film industry was easily linked within six steps to Bacon.

Well, I guess Alf was now linked to Bacon in a way. Even later, I read somewhere that Bacon even started a website and charitable organization based on *Six Degrees*. And I sent a donation.

I, however, never had even one degree of separation from losing Alf.

PART VI

BEN

———◆———

I'M NOT CERTAIN when the idea started to grow in my head or how the seed was first planted, but I couldn't get Carolina's sudden and sheer aloneness out of my thoughts in the days, weeks, and months following Alf's funeral. I talked about it in passing with Virginia when she was home between overseas trips, but she seemed to take a somewhat cavalier attitude, saying, "It's what she signed up for when Alf committed to The Citadel and the Marine Corps. And when she committed to him and the Corps years ago."

I was stunned at Virginia's response and thought she might think differently if she were in Carolina's very solitary shoes. I didn't, however, pursue it further with Virginia—at least not then.

I did return to TR whenever I could get away from Richmond, when Virginia was out of town. Due to my work with Luck Stone, this often meant driving down just for the day or maybe just one night.

My mother, who was also alone for the first time in many years, was pleased with my visits. However, I'll admit that I also hoped to see Carolina. That happened just twice in the first three months or so after Alf's death. On the surface, it seemed she'd moved on, staying in her small apartment and even taking on a few freelance stringer writing jobs with *The Greenville News* and a couple of other Upcountry publications and websites.

When Carolina and I were together those two times, it was with my mom or with her parents, and she seemed more distant than

I'd ever seen her. I attributed this to Alf's death, but it also seemed eerily reminiscent of Alf's stoicism back at The Citadel and beyond.

On one visit back to TR the day after Christmas, with Virginia already back overseas somewhere she couldn't share, when it was just Carolina and me in her apartment's little living room overlooking a parking lot, I finally asked, "So how's it going, my sweet sister-in-law?"

She smiled meekly and seemed to ponder the question before replying, "Am I still your sister-in-law, Ben, if I'm not married to your brother anymore?"

"Of course, Carolina. You'll always be my sister-in-law. And so much more. I hope you know that."

"I do, Ben. But there's this really unfair feeling I have now that, when Alf died, I also lost you and your mom as my family as well.

"But—"

"I know, I know. It doesn't really make sense, and it's not something any of you have said or done. It's just this strange feeling that I'm some sort of an orphan, as well as a widow. Or something like that. I know I still have my parents, but your mother was like a second mom to me, and you, you were like a brother. I'm . . . I'm honestly not sure exactly what I'm saying."

"Well, you're as much a part of our family now as you were when we were growing up and when you two got married. That didn't change, Car."

We looked into each other's eyes, and I think we both noticed that this was the first time I'd ever called her Car, instead of Carolina, in person. I'll never know why I chose that particular conversation to do so, and I'm sure I didn't make a conscious choice. Perhaps it had something to do with a sense of obligation to care for Carolina.

"I know you say it hasn't changed, Ben, but you're not here. Everyone says I still have my parents and, of course, you and your mom, but it's just not the same. I knew when Alf chose to go to The Citadel and into the Marine Corps that I would be alone a lot of the time. I just didn't know it could mean I'd be permanently alone. And I am."

"I'm not going to try to convince you otherwise, but just know that we're all still here in any and all ways. None of us can ever replace Alf for you, but we will always be your family."

Carolina looked at me and nodded, but I could tell her heart was saying that no amount of love from her parents or my mom and me could replace the hole that losing Alf had left in her life. And mine as well, of course.

That conversation and my use of "Car" that late-December day gave me much food for thought on my drive back to Richmond. I'd always loved Carolina, but the definition of my love for her changed the day she chose Alf. It had grown into a brotherly sort of love for a sister.

However, during the drive back to Richmond on the twenty-eighth, I found myself having other sorts of feelings for Carolina. And it went well beyond a teenager's infatuation years earlier.

It's strange to look back on that day and night, considering what I did back in my Richmond apartment; I turned on my laptop at the kitchen counter bar and typed a Google search: "Can a brother marry his dead brother's wife?" What I read over two bottles of Heineken would change my life and the lives of several others forever.

My search revealed a concept called "levirate" marriage. That evening, I read that levirate marriage was very popular in ancient times, when a brother would often marry his dead brother's wife. Back then, it had much to do with the deceased brother's child or children and their inheritances. I found that Deuteronomy 25 said, "If brothers are living together and one of them dies without a son, his widow must not marry outside the family. Her husband's brother shall take her and marry her and fulfill the duty of a brother-in-law to her."

Due to war and other circumstances thought to justify the practice, levirate marriages were practiced in Judaism and Islam, as well as by English royalty and in China, Africa, and beyond. Even in modern times, nomadic cultures and countries like Somalia, Nigeria, and other African countries still sometimes follow levirate-like marriage traditions. Of course, Google also reminded me of the levirate marriage in Shakespeare's *Hamlet*, where Claudius—brother of deceased King Hamlet—marries the widow Gertrude.

The more I read, the more I realized I was seriously considering the concept of some sort of levirate marriage with Carolina that had little relation to its traditional role. I knew in my heart that, for me, it had as much to do with loving Carolina as honoring my brother or ensuring Carolina's future. I smiled to myself when I said out loud in the silent room, "This certainly wouldn't be much ado about nothing."

Early the next morning, I walked into the still-dark kitchen and realized I'd left my laptop on overnight. The Google search screen was the first thing I saw. I made a pot of coffee, sat back down, and continued reading for the half hour I had to spare before heading to a project where we were installing granite counters for a VMI grad's kitchen.

As I drove out to the West End project, I couldn't help but picture Carolina's reaction if I ever talked to her about this admittedly unique idea. I laughed out loud as I passed by Matthew Fontaine Maury's statue, thinking that my unique proposal would certainly be a path and possibly treacherous sailing for the famed "Pathfinder of the Seas."

I didn't talk to Virginia then about my thoughts concerning Carolina, and I wish I had much earlier than I did. I'll love her forever for how she handled what was to come.

On a chilly, early-April day, I returned to Travelers Rest after calling Carolina the night before to make sure she'd be there. I told her I had a question for her. She seemed to hesitate before laughing and said, "Of course, Ben, but can't you just ask me on the phone right now?"

"No, I don't think so, Carolina," I said quickly. "When you hear what I have to say tomorrow, you'll most definitely know why I couldn't do it on the phone."

"Well, now you really have me curious, Ben. You do know you don't have to ask me about asking Virginia to marry you, right? Your mom and I have been telling you for much too long that she's the one for you."

I wasn't sure what to say to that ironic question, so I simply replied, "I'll see you tomorrow, Car." I was finding that I liked the sound of "Car."

The drive back home to TR from Richmond was as familiar to me as the route between home and Lexington had become during my four years at VMI. However, this time was dramatically different, in that I don't remember looking at the passing scenery, which typically enthralled me on both drives.

Virginia was with me on several of the trips to Travelers Rest, and I recalled so much of what we talked about along the way. I realized then that no matter the outcome of my conversation with Carolina, my relationship with Virginia would never be the same.

Though I had called my mom earlier that morning and told her I was coming to town, I went straight to Carolina's apartment without stopping by my house first. She was sitting on her little second-floor balcony, drinking what I knew was a cup of the strong, loose green tea she'd grown to love at Chapel Hill. She stood and waved down to me as I walked to the stairs, but she didn't speak, and I simply returned her wave.

Her front door was open by the time I got to it, and she gave me the familiar hug that had become remarkably similar to the ones my mother had given me all of my life. I'd once tried to read much more into those hugs from Carolina than I knew they likely meant.

"Get in here, Mr. Mysterious," she said, pulling me into the living room with her right hand, which, of course, I immediately noticed held her Citadel miniature. "I couldn't wait for you to get your butt down here and ask me your oh-so-mysterious question. It's so unlike you, Ben."

"Well, like I said, when you hear what I have to ask you, if I even ask you, you will know why I couldn't do it on the phone. Hey, I thought you said you'd put that ring in a closet?"

"Oh, this?" asked Carolina, looking down. "I did put it away, but grabbed it this morning so we could sorta have Alf with us. I guess it's silly, but there you are. Anyway. Let's go back out on the balcony. It's a little cool, but it's sunny and I have that little space heater cranked up for us. Can I get you something to drink?"

"A shot of Virginia Gentleman would be great," I joked. "But a glass of ice water is probably better for now."

"Sure," she said, with wonder in her eyes. "Head on out, and I'll bring it out to you after I make another cup of tea."

When she brought out my glass and her cup, which sported a blue Citadel logo, I asked, "Do you still drink that New Age-y tea you started quaffing in Chapel Hill?"

"Yep," she said, smiling, before sitting down in the wicker chair across from me. "Can't you see it's helping me keep my youthful beauty?" she asked, and running her fingers through her hair.

"You know you never needed to drink anything for me to think you're beautiful, Car," I said, staring straight at her like I hadn't in almost a decade.

Of course, my words and gaze made for an awkward moment, so I decided to plow ahead with what I'd been rehearsing back in Richmond and on the drive down to TR. Still holding her eyes, I took a deep breath and a gulp of water before softly saying, "I think we should marry, Carolina."

She steadily held my gaze, and, God bless her, Carolina's eyes didn't reveal what must have been a great surprise to her. Without blinking, she smiled and said, "I thought you came here with a question, Ben. That seemed like more of a statement." She continued to hold my gaze with eyes that had a glimmer of merriment in them, which matched her widening smile.

"Don't joke with me, Car. I'm dead serious." Of course, the 'dead' wasn't my best choice of words, but she didn't seem to notice. Or at least didn't reveal it in her still smiling eyes and mouth.

"Are you asking me to marry you, Ben, or just saying you think we should? There's a difference."

"Both," I said, taking her hand in mine, relieved that she let me.

"Well, um . . . wow. You can guess this has really caught me off guard, to say the least. I have so many questions. Like this one: why?"

"That's a good one to start with, of course, and I have lots of long answers to that one-word question. If you'll hear me out, I'll try to give you all of the reasons I've worked out for you. For us. But I didn't want this part of it to be a planned speech. It's going to come from the heart."

"Are you sure you don't need that bourbon first, Ben?" she asked, still trying to keep the mood light. "I think maybe I do."

"No, I'm good. Well, as good as I'll ever be before trying to say what I need to say. You ready?"

"As ready as I'll ever be."

"Thanks. Okay. Well, here goes, I guess," I continued, keeping her hand in mine and holding her gaze.

"So, I guess you know I've loved you in different ways for as long as I can remember," I started, seeing her subtle nod. "Of course, that love changed when you chose Alf." Again, a nod. "It never went away, but it was almost like I had to put it into hibernation for what I knew even back then was likely forever.

"I'm sure you realized it was hard being around you two for the rest of high school and those now long, for me, summers. It got easier when we all went off to school, which seemed to make it easier to keep that love for you to myself. And my developing relationship with Virginia over the years helped as well, of course."

The squeeze Carolina gave my hand was my signal to continue.

"When I was with you the day we learned of Alf's death, my only thoughts were of what each of us had lost in our individual ways. You as a wife. Mom as a mother. Me as a brother. And, Virginia, and so many others, as a friend. Of course, we also shared the loss of Alf in other ways. Like his love for all of us separately—and together. And, of course, our country and devotion to it.

"I know that Alf left a last letter for you, and I've very intentionally never asked you what it said, but I wanted to give you another letter that I've never told you about. One he left for me."

I reached into the left back pocket of my jeans and unfolded and smoothed it out with just my shaking left hand before passing it to her. She took it in her right hand without letting go of mine, as if she needed that physical connection to our blood brother as she read his neat handwriting. I know I did.

> Dear Blood Brother,
>
> If you are reading this letter, I've made the ultimate sacrifice for my country, my fellow Marines, and my family. It was my honor.
>
> As you know, I am a man of few words. I have an unusual request of you, and I know as I write this that you will make the right choice, whatever that may be.
>
> Many years ago, Carolina chose me. If you can find it in your heart and your circumstances allow it, I now ask you to choose her. She will need you as I often needed her. Do it for me, brother. Do it for her.
>
> I love you.
>
> Semper Fi,
>
> Alf

As she read the short letter, I kept my eyes on hers and saw them quickly fill with tears. At this, I squeezed her hand even tighter. I knew the words by heart, of course, and I could tell by her eyes and face when she reached the part about me choosing her. That was where she squeezed my hand in return.

She put the letter back on her lap and, after a deep breath in and out, turned to me. "He wrote something similar to me, Ben. I guess you knew that in your heart, didn't you?" At this question, I nodded.

"He referenced you taking care of me. It's still in the Bible in his bedside table, where I found it about a week after his funeral. It's there right now. Would you like to read it, Ben?"

> My Dearest Carolina,
>
> If you are reading this letter, I'm no longer with you in the physical sense. But know that I'll still always be with you in my heart and soul and that we will be reunited someday in whatever heaven our God has created for those we love. Death will not part us.
>
> As I write this, I can't know what Ben's situation will be, but know that I have asked him to take care of you in every way that you may need. He has promised me with his blood that he will do this for me—and you.
>
> Please know that I've loved every minute of my life with you, through good times and bad, when you were always at my side. Thank you for making the choice you did all those years ago. I love you.
>
> Semper Fi,
> Alf

We stared at each other for what seemed like a long time but was probably only thirty seconds. Carolina asked, "What do you think he meant in the letters, Ben?"

I held her gaze and said more of the words I'd been rehearsing. "I've thought about it a lot, Car, and I really think that he wanted us to marry each other, if my—and your—circumstances allowed. And if you would have me, of course. What do you think he meant?"

At that, Carolina stared out into the parking lot and its few small trees before looking up at the sky as if Alf were somehow up there looking down at us. "I don't know, Ben. When I first read his letter to me, I thought that the words—and wording—were strange. But at the time, I guess I thought he was just saying you'd be there if I needed you. And you have been, of course. All of you have been there."

"I think he meant much more than that, Car," I said, taking her chin in my free hand and turning her pretty tear-stained face back to face me. "I think his words to each of us were a request. And, um, maybe permission somehow?"

"Hmm," she said, keeping my gaze after I'd dropped my hand from her chin. "I'm not saying no and I'm not saying yes. Yet. But wouldn't it just be really weird, Ben?"

"Of course. I guess so. But you know me, and I've done my research." I finally smiled slightly. "It's not as weird as you may think.

"I guess the writer in you knows all about Shakespeare's *Hamlet*. But the journalist in you is already thinking that it was just a play, and not real life. Just remember that it was based on both legends and historical facts, as well. And I'm betting you haven't heard of the term 'levirate,' right?"

She shook her head, saying, "No, not at all. What's that?"

"When I first started seriously thinking about this, I put Google to work for me. Something called a levirate marriage was evidently quite frequent in ancient times. It happens when a brother marries his dead brother's wife. Dead brother's widow, I guess."

At that, Carolina flinched, dropped her eyes, and took her hand from mine. "I really think I need that drink now, Ben. This is a lot to process."

"I know. I know. That's why it's taken me so many months to talk to you about it. Back then, levirate marriages were mostly meant to take care of the dead brother's child or children and, possibly, their inheritances of land or whatever." I told her what else I had learned.

"Can you tell I've read—and thought—a lot about it, Car?" I asked, allowing for a small, if brief, smile. "Of course, Google also reminded me of Claudius marrying King Hamlet's widow, Gertrude."

I paused, taking her hand back in mine before asking with a big smile, "So, might you be my Gertrude, Carolina?"

She grinned, and replied, "You sure know how to woo a girl,

Shakespeare."

"Well, I had a lot more time to rehearse the question than you've had to think about an answer. Of course, you don't have to answer right away. Unless it's yes. Or no. I'm thinking you're going to need some time, huh?"

She smiled again before saying, "Uh, yeah. Don't you think?"

"Yep. I figured. Well, take as much or as little time as you need. I know it's pretty damned strange and hard to process."

"To say the least. Have you talked about this with your mom? Or Virginia? What about her?"

"No. Nobody. It's obviously been weighing on me, but I decided very early that it would just be between you and me forever if you said no. Well, I guess it'd be between you, me, and Alf, huh?"

I could tell this last thought gave Carolina pause, but she seemed to recover, asking, "How do you think Virginia would react if I said yes to you, Ben?"

"I'm honestly not sure. I've thought about it a lot, and I think maybe Virginia was what and who Alf was referring to when he wrote of 'circumstances.'"

"Hmmm. I'll bet you're right. But how do you think she'd take it?"

"If I know Virginia, she'd find it in her heart to support me—and us. This is hard for me to say, but I think Virginia has always known that I loved you first. And that I'd choose you over her, if given the chance."

"Oh, that would be so hard for any woman to hear, Ben. Even someone as strong as Virginia."

"I know. Don't you think it's been difficult to even think about the consequences of this?"

"It's hard for me to think about too. And what about your mother?"

"I have no idea. It'd be very trying for me to tell her about what I've been thinking and am now proposing, but—like Virginia—I didn't want anyone else to know if you say no. And I know this seems silly, but I even thought about asking your parents for your hand in marriage."

This made her smile again, and though I'd seriously thought about asking her parents, my confession unintentionally—and thankfully—lightened the mood again. "I'd love to see that," Carolina laughed. "If I do say yes, I'll let you tell 'em."

"Sure. And I'd want you there when I tell my mom. But maybe not Gin."

"I'm not saying yes, Ben. Or no. It's just . . . so sudden. And strange. And loving. Yes. It's loving, Ben."

"Oh, it's all about love, Car. About loving you. But also about loving Alf. And maybe even loving Virginia enough to have unwittingly helped me even get to this point."

"I still can't believe you've kept it inside you for all this time."

"I think I've actually been keeping it inside of me since the day I read Alf's letter, right after the funeral. Heck, in some ways, I would swear I've kept it inside of me since the day you chose Alf."

"Oh, Ben," Carolina said, facing me fully and taking both of my hands in hers. "I wish you wouldn't use 'chose' anymore after all of these years. I know it may have felt like it back then, and it sounds like it still does, but I never felt like I was choosing Alf over you."

Still holding her hands in mine, I asked the question that I'd wanted to ask for years. "What was it then, Car?"

Holding my eyes, which were filled with tears for the first time that morning, she said, "I thought about it a lot when it was happening. Especially when things changed between the three of us and you seemed so hurt by my decision, if that's what you call it. I never saw it so much of a choice I made as that I was chosen by Alf."

"But I chose you too, Car," I said quickly and somewhat defensively.

At that, she took her hands from mine and held them up between us as if defending herself from my words, saying, "Hold on now, Ben. Hear me out, okay?

"What I mean—and this may be hard to hear so many years later—is that Alf seemed to be choosing me in a way you hadn't. Or at least, back then, in a way that you couldn't or didn't express like he did that day—and earlier days that summer as well."

"Wow, I've never really thought of it that way. Man, I wish I'd asked you about this a long time ago."

"Until your brother died, I'm not sure that would have been the answer I'd given you. I'm not sure I really knew either."

"Well, I'm glad you told me today. Does it affect how you might answer me now?"

"No, not really. I guess it could be viewed as some sort of second chance for me. And for you too, huh? But saying yes—or no—isn't as simple as one door closing and another one opening. It goes much deeper than that for both of us, doesn't it?"

"Yes, it does, Car. I think that's why it took me this long to ask you. And maybe there needed to be some space and time between us after losing Alf. And maybe even for my mom too."

"I know. I can't help thinking about your mom in all of this. I have to be honest, Ben. This is a lot for me to process. Were you planning on talking about this with your mom while you're here?"

"Oh, no, Car. As I told you, this will only be between you and me—and Alf—if you say no. I promise."

"Okay. Yeah, I forgot you told me that already," she said, staring into the distance. "Like I said, it's a lot to think about, for sure."

"I know, I know. I've had months to think about it, and you've had mere minutes. Take all the time you want."

With that, we both got up and carried our cups back to her kitchen counter. I turned awkwardly to give her a hug, but Carolina— bless her—held me tightly, as if she were hugging me for both her and for Alf for what I'd just done—and asked.

CAROLINA

———●——○——●———

BEN LEFT MY apartment about eleven that morning and I stayed inside to make another cup of tea before heading back onto my balcony. Sitting in my wicker chair, I looked up, smiled, and asked out loud to the ceiling fan, "Did that just happen?"

In my mind and in my heart, the warm breeze and soft whir from the ceiling fan seemed to respond in Alf's voice, "Yes."

I couldn't help but chuckle, remembering Alf had told me he'd be with me beyond that death-do-us-part thing. *And here he is,* I thought as I sipped my tea and began to think in earnest about Ben's strange proposal.

In some ways, it seemed so simple. Say yes and almost immediately lose much of the loneliness that had come so suddenly with Alf's death. Of course, in the short time we were married, I'd grown used to Alf being away, but that was more like being alone temporarily. Since his death and knowing he wasn't coming back to me, sheer and total loneliness had literally twice brought me to my knees.

Would saying yes to Ben remove that loneliness? Would it also honor Alf's apparent request that Ben take Alf's place if circumstances allowed? Plus, in his note to me, Alf commented about Ben being there if he was no longer there for me.

However, there were also many logical reasons for saying no. First, there was simply the sheer strangeness of it all and what people would think of me—and us. What people thought had never been a big concern for me, but I'd never fathomed pursuing something like what Ben was, literally, proposing.

I also wondered whether saying no would relieve Ben from what he probably saw as a duty to his brother —and, to me, I guess. Plus, I knew that he cared deeply for Virginia. Saying no to him would allow them to continue to pursue their growing and loving relationship and what I always assumed would be their marriage.

I needed to talk through this with someone, and, ironically, that someone really would have been Alf. I knew Ben had told me that if my decision was no, nobody else would ever know about this. But he hadn't specifically asked me to not speak with anyone about it. Without Alf as my confidante, I found myself thinking that the person I'd needed to talk to was Alf and Ben's mother.

I went back inside with a sudden hunger that I didn't notice until I was walking toward the kitchen. I'd always found that chopping ingredients or really any kind of food preparation or cooking was meditative for me. That is especially true when I need time to think. And this was certainly one of those times.

I decided to make gazpacho, thinking that all the time cutting the various vegetables would help me sort my jumbled thoughts. My roommate at Chapel Hill studied abroad in Barcelona for a semester and returned ready to make gazpacho practically every other day. I thus became a big fan of the chilled Spanish delicacy as well.

Thanks to my love of vegetables, I had most of the ingredients in my Frigidaire, and I smiled as I pulled out a tomato, a cucumber, and a half-used bunch of celery, tearing off a stalk and putting the rest of it back in the fridge. After pulling out my worn wooden cutting board and my favorite Henckels knife, I started to slice the celery, then realized that I'd never fixed gazpacho for Alf. I then found myself wondering if Ben liked it. I was surprised I didn't know.

Growing up, I remember their mom telling me that Alf and Ben would come in from the yard at separate times on weekend mornings and ask for the exact same thing for lunch, swearing to her that they hadn't talked to each other about it first. I was at many of those lunches back then and missed those simple meals—and times. I smiled, thinking that I was pretty certain Alf and Ben hadn't asked for gazpacho on those long-ago weekends. I seem to recall it was often mac and cheese, which I'd made for Alf several times. It was our comfort food. I'm not sure I'd ever be comfortable making it again.

After I chopped the colorful ingredients, I kept back a little tomato and put everything else in the blender, running it for a good two minutes to make sure everything was smooth before pouring it into one of my bright-yellow Fiesta bowls and topping it with the remaining chopped tomato and some dried cilantro, since I didn't have any fresh stems in the fridge.

I took my bowl and a glass of iced tea back out onto the balcony, sitting at the Pier One table Alf and I bought when we were furnishing our little cottage at Camp Lejeune.

As I'd hoped, the gazpacho preparation had calmed my mind enough to revisit Ben's proposal. Between slurped spoonfuls of soup, I found myself staring skyward as if Alf were looking down on me again and could telepathically tell me what to do.

I softly said, "Help me, Alf," but I knew the answer wouldn't come from him. In a way, he'd already given me his answer by asking Ben to pursue this. But that honestly wasn't enough for me.

As I sat there drinking the last of my iced tea, I returned to my earlier thought that I really wanted to talk to their mom. I knew Ben had gone over to their house after he left, but I didn't know how long he was staying before driving back to Richmond.

I walked back inside, grabbed the phone from the wall, and called their house using one of only four numbers I'd stored in my phone since moving back home when Alf deployed. The second one was for my parents' home next to the Marshalls, the third was for Ben, and the fourth, which was number one on speed dial, was still Alf.

Marge answered after the first ring, and I realized I hadn't really considered what I was going to say. I hesitated, then said, "Oh hey, Marge. Is Ben there?"

"Hi, Carolina. It's great to hear your voice. No, I'm afraid you just missed him. He ate a quick bowl of mac and cheese, then headed back to Richmond. It was certainly Ben's shortest stay that I can remember. He said he'd stopped by to see you first, but didn't say why."

"I was just thinking while I was doing the dishes that he seemed really quiet. What'd you say to him, Car?" she asked. "Don't you go upsetting my boy," she continued, with a gentle mocking tone in her voice.

"The only thing I said was that he needed to go see you before heading home."

She laughed, saying, "Well, you know he'd never miss a chance at my mac and cheese. I did miss seeing Virginia this visit. She's a keeper."

"I know, I know," I replied awkwardly, thinking about what I wanted to discuss with her. "Hey, I was wondering if you were going to be around the house later this afternoon. I'd love to come by and catch up a bit."

"Of course, Carolina. I'd really like that. You know I always have time for you. Why don't I make up a batch of iced tea and we can have it out on the back deck? It's not too hot out there later in the afternoon. Say about five?"

"That'd be great," I said, thinking that I wasn't sure I could wait that long. Or that I might not have the courage to go at all by five o'clock.

BEN

———◆———

THE SHORT DRIVE over to my mom's from Carolina's apartment gave me time to let out the long sigh that I didn't know had been building since I left Richmond. Whatever Carolina's answer, the question that I'd inevitably marched toward had been asked.

I walked in the back door to our kitchen and immediately knew that my mother had made mac and cheese. There was something about melted cheese that made me think of my childhood—and, of course, Alf and Carolina. How many times had the four of us sat at the kitchen counter where my mother now stood smiling and shared bowls of steaming pasta and processed cheese—and our days?

"Hey, son," she said, enveloping me in a hug that felt strong and smelled good. "You're just in time. Y'all always seemed to know when I'd drained the pasta and the mac and cheese was almost ready."

"That was always me and Carolina, Mom. Alf wanted to stay outside and play. I swear he would have skipped lunch if you'd let him."

"Well, how come both of you would often come in sometime in the morning and say you wanted the same thing for Saturday lunch?"

"True. True. But odds were we'd both ask for mac and cheese a lot of the time, right?"

"Good point, Ben, but you two often seemed to have one mind."

"It was pretty amazing wasn't it? Remember that time we each wrote those papers for classes back at school and he wrote about the end of football and I wrote about the end of war? Or do I have that backwards?"

"No, that's right. I'll never forget that. You were back here for Christmas break and I asked about your classes. I think it was the first semester of your junior years, if I recall correctly. Anyway, that's when it came out what you'd both written. I've told a lot of people that story and a few others about you two growing up and sharing the same thoughts and stuff."

After she served the steaming and pungent bowls, we sat at the counter in silence. If I knew my mom, she was thinking about all of the times she had made lunch for Alf and me—and, more than likely, Carolina.

"Do you miss him more at times like this, Mom?" I asked, interrupting the quiet that often ensues when you get lost in comfort food and thoughts.

"Of course," she said, putting her fork in the bowl and turning to me. "It's definitely harder when we're doing something we used to share together. Like this."

"I know. Over at Car's, we were sitting out on her balcony, and I was thinking about how much Alf liked summers. I didn't say anything to her, though."

"I can guarantee you she was thinking the same thing, son. She won't say it, but I'd swear that Carolina misses us as a group almost as much as she misses Alf individually. It's like she not only lost him but also lost you and me in some ways as well. I guess Alf was our link and our glue."

"I know what you mean. We may never get that back, huh?" I asked, thinking how much I was hoping to change that.

The rest of lunch passed quickly, and my mom was surprised and disappointed when I said I had to get back to Richmond. "But you just got here, Ben."

"I know, but I just needed to talk to Carolina about something. I'll stay longer next time."

I left her at the back door, promising to call when I got back to my apartment. Of course, my drive back was filled with thoughts of

Carolina and what she must be thinking. My proposal had certainly changed her weekend. And, quite possibly, her life. Again.

CAROLINA

———○———

IT WAS ONLY a half mile to the Marshalls, so I decided to walk to clear my head as best I could before talking to Marge. My route would have normally taken me right past my old house, but I walked around the block to the other side of Marge's house instead, just in case my parents were outside doing yardwork, as they often did come early evening.

As I'd done hundreds of times growing up, I went straight to the back door and entered without knocking. Marge was at the kitchen table, where there'd always been four chairs and still were. She looked so alone sitting there, glancing up from her steaming teacup before standing to give me a hug and asking, "I know I promised iced tea on the phone, but do you want some hot tea instead?"

"Sure," I said. "But I can get it."

"Thanks, the kettle should still be hot, I think, and the bags are right there."

I quickly made my tea and returned to the table, sitting across from her. I wondered if I'd chosen that seat to keep my distance—or to be able to look her straight in the eyes. As I sat down with a sigh, I realized it had been where Alf always sat.

"I'm game to stay inside where it's cool, if you are."

"That'd be great, Marge."

"I'm sorry you missed Ben. Did you have something else to tell him? He seemed so mysterious about his visit with you."

"He didn't say anything about why he came to see me, right?"

"No, not at all," she quickly responded, looking at me with a quizzical look on her face.

"Well, you'll know why he didn't say anything when I tell you what I'm about to share. But I must ask for your word that you won't tell anyone else we've talked about this if I ask you not to. Including Ben and my parents. Okay?"

She held my gaze and said, "Of course, Car. You know you've always been like a daughter to me. What's bothering you? And what did Ben say that obviously has you so upset?"

I looked down at my hands, twirling the Citadel miniature that I was still wearing, then glancing to where my engagement ring and wedding band once were. And, finally, I looked up and simply said, "Ben has asked me to marry him, Marge. And I don't know what to do."

Without hesitation, my dear mother-in-law got up from her chair, came around to me, pulled me to my feet, and took me in her arms. And, with that, I had the answer I think I'd known all along. Maybe even before Ben had asked the question.

After the longest hug I ever remember receiving from anyone, Marge released me, and I sat back down a different person. She went back to her side of the table and sat as well, reaching across to take my hands before asking, "Did Ben say why he asked you this, Carolina?"

"Yes. He brought a letter that Alf had written to him, which seemed to ask Ben to take care of me if we lost him. Or something like that. I guess it was sorta like what Alf had said in that letter I showed you after the funeral saying that Ben would take care of me."

"I remember that letter, Car, but I never knew he wrote to Ben as well."

"Yeah. Ben's hands were shaking so badly when he handed me that letter. And also when he asked me to marry him. Um, unless I misunderstood you, you think I should say yes, right?"

"I do. Yes, Car. I really, really do. I hope that hug told you that. In some ways, I think it's the only answer you can give, don't you?"

"But what about Virginia?"

"Hmm. I can't believe I just mentioned Ben marrying Virginia on the phone with you. If I'd only known. But I think you should trust that Ben has thought this through. Did he say anything about already talking to Virginia?"

"He hasn't. He'd really anguished over it, and I can't imagine what he's gone through before coming to see me this morning. And popping that question."

"I know what you mean. Well, what did he say about Virginia? I know how much he thinks of her. We all love her."

"Well, Ben said that if I said no, we wouldn't have to tell anyone, and it could just stay between the two of us. I thought about that before calling you, and that's why I said you may have to keep this to yourself as well. Ben also said that if I said yes, he would tell Virginia on his own."

"Hmm. Well, what does all of this have you thinking?"

"It has me thinking way too much is what it has me doing, Marge. I feel like, either way, my answer is going to hurt someone. And I can't help being mad at Alf, in some ways, for putting us all into this situation."

"Oh, Car. Please don't be mad at Alf. What he'd asked of his brother very likely allowed him to die in some sort of peace, knowing you'd be okay. Like any Marine—and husband, son, brother, and friend—I know that Alf always seemed concerned with the possibility of his own death and those he'd leave behind. I can't help but think that this was part of that process and even his planning. You know he was a planner."

I smiled at that before responding, "But don't you think it'd be really, really strange for me to marry my dead husband's brother—and his twin, at that. Ben said something about it being a being a practice in many cultures from long ago. He said it's called a levirate marriage."

"I don't know about any of that, but my heart is responding more than my head. I do know—and so do you—that Ben has always loved you. And he loved Alf in ways that go way beyond being blood brothers. I heard them say this more than once."

"I know, I know. And I'll bet you didn't know that I actually became a so-called blood brother with them as well, so long ago. It's just that it still seems really weird somehow. What do you think my parents will think? And everybody else in town?"

"Well, I know your parents want what is best for you. And that they would support you whatever you decide. You can't worry about everyone else. You know that in your heart, Carolina. You need to go with your heart."

"Well, I did once before, and it broke Ben's heart. I don't want to do that again to Ben or to someone else."

"I don't think you would if you decided to say no, Carolina. If I know Ben, he's thought this to death and will find a way to move forward, again, whatever your decision."

"But you really think I should say yes, don't you?" I asked, looking down at our intertwined hands.

She squeezed my hand firmly, including my Citadel ring, before saying, "Yes, sweet Carolina, I think you should say yes. Again."

We finished our tea in silence, and as I got up and started for the door, Marge said, "And by the way, I'd never heard you'd become a blood brother—or sister, I guess—with them. I love that, Car."

I turned around at the back door, looked at Marge, smiled, and asked, "Do you know if Ben likes gazpacho?"

I headed out Marge's back door feeling like a very different person from the one who entered a half hour earlier. This time, I did walk by my parents' house, where—ironically—I went to the front door and rang the bell.

My mother answered and gave me a quick hug and a confused look at the surprise visit, as well as my not coming around to the back door. She turned and, over her shoulder, said, "We're in the kitchen waiting on the meatloaf."

I gave my dad a quick hug just before he asked, "To what do we owe this surprise pleasure, Miss Carolina?"

He'd called me "Miss Carolina" since I was a child with more of a penchant for white baseballs than my mom's white pearls. I always assumed he was hoping I'd grow into his little princess instead of the tomboy I was until my mid-teens.

I was most definitely a daddy's girl, and I found myself thinking that I was now a daddy's woman as well. I'd never forget how he and my mom were there for me when Alf died.

"Hey, Dad. That meatloaf smells amazing, as always."

"Can you stay for dinner?" he asked, holding up a third plate he must have pulled out of the cabinet when he heard me come in the front door.

"No. I was just walking back home from next door and thought I'd stop and say, 'Hey.'"

"Well, hey, then," he said, looking disappointed as he put the plate back in the cabinet. "What are you doing tonight that allows you to resist my meatloaf and your mother's mashed potatoes with gravy?"

"Oh, I rented *The Fellowship of the Ring* from Blockbuster again yesterday, and I fell asleep halfway through it last night. I'm heading back to make some popcorn to see if I can finish it off without dozing off. Again. I think it's really because I almost have it memorized, you know? I will take a couple of slices of that meatloaf and some spoonfuls of mashed potatoes and gravy, if you can spare 'em."

"Of course," Dad said, already reaching back into the cabinet to retrieve the plate. "I'll cover it, and you can just heat it up during the movie."

After he fixed my plate, covered it with plastic wrap, and put it in an Ingles paper bag, I hugged them goodbye. I wanted to be alone with my popcorn, Frodo Baggins, my meatloaf and mashed potatoes, and my thoughts about Ben's proposal.

BEN

◆

THE DRIVE BACK to Richmond was very different than my drive down to TR. The weight that I'd been carrying for months concerning Alf's request and whether or not I could ask Carolina to marry me had been lifted, but now the wait for Carolina to decide had become a new weight to shoulder.

Normally, when I was driving alone, I listened to audiobooks. I was halfway through Tolkien's *Fellowship of the Ring*, but the sixth CD sat unplayed in the passenger seat for my drive down and my return to Richmond. The chatter in my brain about very different rings and other things was the only soundtrack I seemed capable of listening to for now.

Strangely, I felt like I had already fulfilled my brother's request. It was now up to Carolina. I knew that Alf's desire that I take care of her went deeper than simply asking her to marry me. He'd meant for us to carry on the life that had been taken from him—and Carolina.

I could never fill my brother's very different shoes and boots, but I realized as I drove that this had not really been his goal or wish at all. Maybe he was telling both Carolina and me that he wanted us to continue life. I shook my spinning head as the light along I-95 faded, though I felt like the light was becoming brighter as well.

Back in my apartment, I wondered what Carolina was doing at that very moment. She was one of only five numbers in my phone's autodial, and I had to smile as I pressed the number one. The others were my mom, Virginia's, and Virginia's mom just up Monument Avenue. And Alf's.

Carolina answered after the second ring with a sleepy-sounding "Hello?"

"Hey, Car, it's Ben. Whatcha doing?"

"Falling asleep again to *The Fellowship of the Ring* with a half-eaten bowl of popcorn. How 'bout you?"

After quickly recovering from the coincidence of the film she was watching, I said, "Well, I'm heating up some leftover mac and cheese my mother sent back with me. It's my second bowl today. And, of course, I'm thinking about you, and this morning."

"Oh, me too, Ben. Quite the day for both of us, huh?"

"Well, what's your decision?" I quipped.

"Hey, now. You said I could take as long as I wanted, right?"

"Yeah. Don't worry. I was, um, sorta kidding. You know I'll wait for as long as you need, and you know I'll understand your decision either way."

"Thanks, Ben. You were always so good to me—and us—that way. Thank you. And whatever I decide, thank you for asking me and for honoring your brother's wishes of you. I'm not sure every brother could—or would—do it."

"I never doubted asking you, once I made the decision. But that still doesn't mean it was easy. I'm not sure I could have even gone this far if it was anyone but you, Car."

"That's so sweet, Ben. You do know I love you like a brother, right?"

Of course, that question, coming from her—especially that day—gave me pause. She finally filled the silence by awkwardly continuing, "I, um, hope that came out the right way, Ben. It just sorta leapt out of my sleep-addled mouth.

"I . . . I guess what I mean to say is that I grew to love you like a brother from the time we were teenagers—and even before then, really. And that love just grew and grew once Alf and I started dating, even if you didn't know it and I didn't always show you. It was almost like you became a brother for me too—the brother I never had."

I waited to see if she'd say more. When she didn't, I asked, "So, are you saying it'd be weird to be married to someone you think of as a brother?"

"Oh, no, Ben," she quickly responded. "Not at all. I'm really just saying that my love for you is already there and, that, if I do say yes to you, it might take some time for me to love you in the way I grew to love Alf in the time we were together—and apart. Does that make sense?"

"I think so. I guess I've been selfishly thinking more about myself and my role in all of this. I'm sorry for not realizing better how this all must feel for you. I know you miss Alf so much, and I'm not trying to replace him in any way. You know that, right, Car?"

"Oh, I know it Ben. I don't think Alf was asking you to be his replacement at all. I will honestly always believe that he was thinking of both of us—and not just me—when he wrote those letters. Does that make sense?"

"Yes. I was actually thinking the same thing on the drive home. Along with a lot of other stuff. You too, I'll bet."

"Yeah. Even when I was awake, I wasn't really watching the movie. It's funny, I have the movie on pause, and Elijah Wood is frozen on the screen. And he sorta looks like Alf—and you."

I laughed, saying, "I take that as a compliment, Car."

"It is. But Alf always had bigger ears than you," she laughed, trying to lighten our moods.

"Well, I'll let you get back to Frodo Baggins and his big ears. Call me tomorrow if you want to."

"Same to you. I think we have quite the Sunday ahead of us, huh?"

"Yep. I hope I didn't ruin your weekend, Carolina."

"Oh, no. Though it certainly wasn't the weekend I was expecting when you called Friday night."

"Yeah, I know. At least I had been living with this for the last few months, so I'd kinda gotten used to the concept. You couldn't see it—or me—coming."

"I can't imagine what the last few months for you have been like, trying to decide if, when, and how to pop the question."

"Good point." I smiled. "I guess I never thought how popping the question, as you say, would go."

"If I say no, Ben, do you think you'll ask Virginia to marry you someday?"

Because I'd thought about this a lot, I quickly responded, "Yes. I do. But . . . I don't want that to affect your answer in any way, Car. Okay?"

"Oh, how can it not, Ben? It definitely complicates already complicated matters for me. It'd be like I was your second choice and—"

I interrupted her mid-sentence to say something I wished I'd said back in her apartment that morning. "Hold on, Car. I need to tell you something that I planned on telling you this morning. But I thought I'd put enough on your platter, so I didn't. This is going to be hard—maybe for both of us—but here goes.

"No matter your decision, you should know that you would not be my second choice. Ever. From the day you and Alf became a couple, and, really, even before that, you were always the one for me. My first choice. You remained that way through the rest of high school, VMI, and beyond to today. Even when you and Alf got married.

"I believe that, deep inside, you knew that. So did Alf, I think. And so does my mom, for sure. She always has.

"And this is going to be very hard for me to say, and I know God may strike me down and I'd deserve it, but the day we learned Alf died, a part of me found solace in knowing you were still in my life, even though I'd lost my brother. Please don't hate me for it, Car. I couldn't bear it."

I could tell she'd been holding her breath on the other end of the line before sighing deeply. "Oh, sweet Ben. I could never hate you. That may be one of the most loving things I've ever heard, actually. It's . . . it's just hard to process right now. It's a lot."

"I know, I know. I'm sorry. I just needed you to hear it. I wish I could have told you in person this morning."

"I'm actually glad you didn't, Ben. That might have been too much."

"Thanks for saying that, Car. I can't help but feel selfish—and guilty—that Alf's death allowed me to reveal my love for you."

"Whew. Okay. I think that's truly enough for tonight, don't you, Ben?"

"Me too. I hope it was okay to tell you that. It was hard."

"Oh, I know. But know that I receive it with the love you intended."

"Thank you, Car. Just know that you were always my first choice. Good night."

"Night," she said, softly hanging up her phone.

I fell asleep picturing her in her bedroom, which I'd only seen from her living room. Was she thinking of me? Of Alf?

CAROLINA

———•——○——•———

I COULDN'T WATCH any more of *The Fellowship of the Ring* after I hung up with Ben. Not that I watched much before I fell asleep and was awakened by his call. My thoughts were obviously elsewhere. I finished the rest of my popcorn and, with Frodo still frozen on the screen, heated up the meatloaf and mashed potatoes in my microwave, and took it out to my balcony.

It was a humid and cloudy night, with a wisp of a warm spring breeze joining with my ceiling fan to make it a comfortable early-April evening. I smiled at the thought that my dad somehow knew I needed comfort food on this night.

I spent the next hour replaying the two conversations with Ben, as well as the short one with his mom—Alf's mom. And then, in my head, I had the conversation with Alf that I realized I really needed to have.

I thought I knew how Alf wanted me to answer Ben's proposal. Didn't he say as much in his letter to me? And in his letter to Ben? But what Alf couldn't have known was that Ben and Virginia would grow into the couple they now were and that, in some ways, Alf's request had forced Ben to choose between Virginia and me.

Ben had left Alf's letter to him, and it was still on the side table beside my little love seat. I picked it up and sat where I'd first read it. As I read it again, slowly, I heard Alf's voice in every word.

I returned the letter to the table, still unfolded, and wiped away the tears that had been building. And then, I heard Alf say as clearly as if he was sitting beside me, *"He has promised me with his blood that he will do this for me—and you."*

And, with Alf by my side, I knew my answer.

BEN

———◆———

I WOKE AT six with Alf's voice in my head. I'd been dreaming of his funeral, hearing those rings crashing repeatedly on his coffin. Alf said, *"Do it for me, brother. Do it for her,"* waking me with a start.

Sitting up in bed, looking around the room as if I'd see Alf standing there, smiling down at me, I loudly said, "I did it, brother, damn it. Now it's up to her."

I pulled on the T-shirt I'd thrown to the floor the night before, went to the kitchen, turned on the coffee maker that I'd filled earlier with water and coffee grounds, and stared out my window to Monument Avenue as the coffee dripped just enough for me to pour that first dark half cup. The *Times-Dispatch* delivery guy was nice enough to throw the papers onto my little balcony, so I didn't have to go outside to the front entrance.

I always went straight to the sports pages every morning to see, if I didn't already know, whether my two Braves teams had won. The Shields family had held season tickets at the Diamond, just a mile or so from their house, ever since it opened in 1985, and Virginia told me that her great-grandfather and grandfather had season tickets at old Parker field before that.

It was inevitable that I'd become a Richmond Braves and Atlanta Braves fan once I started going to games with Virginia and her family. This morning's paper brought the news that the R-Braves had beaten the Norfolk Tides 2–1 down at Harbor Stadium in a pitching duel, while the A-Braves had beaten the Mets 10–8 in a homer-laden slugfest.

I knew I needed to spend the day distracted from thinking about Carolina back in TR. I thought about calling Virginia's mom and Mr. and Mrs. Shields to see if they were going to be around later in the day. I was obviously looking for practically anything to keep my mind occupied.

Whenever I had moments like this in the past, including during the stresses at VMI, which sometimes brought me to my knees, I went for a run. So, I changed out of my boxers into running shorts, put on my well-worn New Balances, and walked out my building's front door onto still-quiet Monument Avenue. Virginia always said she loved Sunday mornings in the Fan, and I'd grown to enjoy them as well. This was especially true when she was back home and out of harm's way, but today I was on my own.

I walked up Monument to Jackson's towering statue, turned left on Boulevard, and then started a slow jog toward Byrd Park on Boulevard, already thinking about running around Shields Lake. I'd never asked Virginia or anyone else if the lake's name had any connection with their family, but I often gravitated toward the small lake, which was really more like two ponds divided by Amelia Street, when I went for a run in the park.

After running over the quiet Downtown Expressway, I passed between Boat Lake and the tennis courts where Arthur Ashe had played and thought of his statue further up the street from my apartment. What a different world Ashe experienced in Richmond— both good and bad, of course, but isn't that often the case in life?

When I got to Shields Lake, I turned right, like I always did, enjoying the warm breeze in my face as I made my way counterclockwise around the water, completing my typical two loops. Normally, when I got back to Swan Lake Drive where I'd begun my two loops, I made my way back to Monument.

But today I decided to extend my run a bit by circling in the other direction for one more loop around the lake. And once again, I noticed something that I noticed whenever I ran—or drove—back from where I'd come. Everything seemed new and quite different than just a few minutes earlier. Suddenly, I wondered if this run around Shields Lake had me running away from Virginia Shields—and toward Carolina Stone.

I weaved my way back home using Meadow, Grove, and Robinson instead of my normal direct return route along Boulevard. I even went out of my way to see if Virginia's mom or grandparents might be doing some early yardwork in the shade of their sprawling front yard. Nobody was outside, and it was still too early to knock, so I continued the two-block walk east to my apartment building

I always kept a pitcher of iced coffee in my fridge for a shot of post-run caffeine, so I poured a glass over ice, added some skim milk, and walked through the French doors onto the balcony to finish scanning the newspaper.

The front page led with yet another article about the situation in Iraq, and as always, I didn't read anything other than the dire headline and the deaths involved on both sides. I knew it was quite possible that Virginia was over there, coming to the end of her day, facing known and unknown enemies. I'd chosen to avoid reading about our continued war on terrorism in places near and far, many of which Virginia knew all too well.

After taking the last gulp of my iced coffee, my Timex watch told me it was just 8:15. But it didn't tell me how to make time move faster. I was still staring at my watch when the phone rang.

CAROLINA

⸺●⸺○⸺●⸺

I WOKE WITH a start in my sunlit bedroom, still hearing Alf's voice in my head. I had assumed I wouldn't sleep well and that I would get up early, but when I looked at my clock, I was surprised to see it was almost eight. Well, 7:50 to be exact.

Alf had always kept our simple little digital clock on his side of the bed, and I'd left it there. For some reason, I decided to move over to his side of the bed and, with another start, found it felt warm. I figured I must have been sleeping on his side of the bed sometime before I awoke. But it was still strange.

The last words I remember Alf whispering in my dream were, *"Death will not part us,"* and it had been as if he were lying next to me. In the early mornings, when Alf would leave me in bed back at Camp Lejeune, he'd whisper, "Semper fi, Carolina." Then, he quietly crawled out of bed, put on his fatigues, and laced up his boots.

I moved over to the still-warm spot beside me, staring at the clock as it changed from one minute to the next. When it flicked to 7:55, I rolled back over to what I still saw as my side of the bed, swung my feet to the floor, and got out of bed, knowing what I needed to do.

I filled my tea kettle and leaned against the counter, waiting for it to boil, so I could carry a cup of tea out onto the balcony, where I hoped it might still be cool despite sleeping in. Without really thinking about it, I grabbed the portable phone from the wall on my way outside.

I pulled the chain for the ceiling fan, which stirred up the quickly warming air just enough to make me want to stay. Glancing at my watch, I saw it was 8:15. I dialed Ben's number, and he answered with a breathless "Hello" after the first ring.

And I simply said, "Yes."

BEN

◆

CAROLINA AND I were married on a sunny July day in Clearview Baptist Church, where she'd married Alf. We planned a simple wedding, inviting only twenty people to the short service and reception. We opted for no bridesmaids or groomsmen, with Car's father giving her away, as he had for her marriage to Alf. Nick Adams was kind enough to be my best man, appropriately combining my Virginia and South Carolina worlds, as I saw it.

Virginia was there that day as well, as was her mom, Beth. I know it must have been difficult for Virginia, and even for Beth, but I knew they would be there. In fact, if I recall correctly, my sweet Virginia was the first person to breezily hug Carolina at the reception. Watching them, I could almost hear Robbin Thompson singing "Sweet Virginia Breeze," and I thought how Virginia, the person and the state, would always be part of my life. And in thinking of Thompson's "red bird" riff in the song, so would cardinals:

> *I've got a red bird singin on my window sill,*
> *I know everything will be all right,*
> *Livin in the Sweet Virginia Breeze.*

The Wednesday before the wedding, we met with Clearview's longtime minister, Kevin Caudill, to discuss our vows. We decided on the traditional wording he suggested for both of us.

As we were walking through the short ceremony with the minister, Carolina said, "Do you remember that Alf and I didn't include 'til death do us part' in our ceremony, Ben? I've thought a lot about that over the years, wondering if Alf had some sort of premonition or something. I even remember joking about it with him after we'd met with Pastor Caudill."

I'd honestly forgotten about that choice. Of course, I couldn't help but also wonder what Alf had been thinking when he asked Car if those words could be omitted.

So, exactly a year after we lost Alf, I repeated these words to dear Carolina and to the small group of friends and family we'd invited to share the day with us:

> *I, Ben, take you, Carolina, to be my wife, to have and to hold from this day forward, for better, for worse, for richer, for poorer, in sickness and in health, to love and to cherish, according to God's holy law, in the presence of God I make this vow.*
>
> *Til death do us part.*

After our vows, Pastor Caudill quickly finished the rest of the ceremony. We had our post-wedding party at Soby's, just like Alf and Carolina's larger reception. Car, our mothers, and I once again kept the food simple, with passed hors d'oeuvres before a simple dinner. We gave everyone a choice of steak or crab cakes for their entrée, with both Car and I opting for the crab cakes as a sort of homage to Alf and Charleston.

At nine o'clock sharp, my mother came to get us for our "grand" exit while most of the guests were still there. After hugging and saying goodbye to the Stones, though we'd see them back in TR the following morning, Carolina and I hugged my mother—and I felt that the three of us shared a moment with Alf. As if she knew what I was thinking, my mom looked at both of us in turn and said, "Alf is here with us. I just know it."

Car and I walked down the stairs into the main part of Soby's and out into the courtyard, where we were immediately showered with rice by everyone who had gone outside ahead of us. We held hands as we passed between our guests and onto Main Street.

After making sure it was okay with Carolina to spend her second wedding night in the old Poinsett Hotel, I had reserved one of the suites, so it was a short walk across the street to our first night as a married couple. Car and I had already checked in, but unfortunately I had left our room key back at our table at Soby's. We walked up to the reception desk and I said, "Hi, we're the Marshalls and we've lost our room key."

The smiling receptionist made a new one for us and handed it to me, nodding at Carolina's pretty white dress and saying, "Congratulations, Mr. and Mrs. Marshall." Incredibly, it was at that moment I realized that Carolina had never changed her last name back to Stone. I turned to her, kissed her lightly on the cheek, held her gaze, and said, "I love you, Mrs. Marshall."

EPILOGUE: BEN

◆

WHEN I LEFT for VMI more than twenty years ago, I could never have imagined the life I'd lead and the people I would meet and love—and lose.

I also couldn't have remotely fathomed falling in love with another cadet and fellow graduate, who would go on to fight the global war on terror that started on that terrible September morning and that may never end.

Of course, given our chosen colleges, I guess losing my brother was always in the back of my mind as we marched our way through VMI, The Citadel, and beyond. However, who could have imagined I'd one day marry his widow and move back home to our beloved Upcountry?

I've returned alone to Alf's gravesite in TR quite often. And, of course, my mom and Carolina sometimes join me. The three of us went to the cemetery the morning of our wedding.

And without exception thus far, rain or shine, on September 11 a small platoon of us marches forth to Mountain View Memorial Park to be with Alf. The group always includes myself, Carolina, my mom, and Car's wonderful parents, the Stones, but we're often joined by many of Alf's brothers- and sisters-in-arms, and, as often as she can be there, my beloved Virginia. I'll keep going as long as I'm able.

Those of us with rings from military schools—including Carolina with her Citadel miniature, which she now wears just once a year—

kneel at Alf's grave, look each other in the eye, and bring our hands crashing down on that cold granite tombstone. I always hope they hear it in Iraq.

As it says on Virginia's state flag and on many VMI rings, "*Sic semper tyrannis.*" Thus, always, to tyrants.

ACKNOWLEDGMENTS

THE SEEDS OF my first novel, *Virginia's Ring*, were planted in the shadows of The Citadel in Charleston, South Carolina, during lunch with Pat Conroy, Citadel Class of 1967. While sitting at a corner table at one of my favorite Charleston restaurants, Slightly North of Broad (SNOB), the famed author of *The Lords of Discipline* and many other bestsellers casually commented, "I think someone should write the VMI novel, and I think you should do it, Lynn."

Though it took me several years of carved-out writing time, *Virginia's Ring* was released in paperback in 2014 and in hardback in 2018. It's since sold thousands of copies. During the process of writing *Virginia's Ring* (and *Carolina's Ring* as well) I both thanked and cursed Pat for the original idea.

Pat knew about the concept of *Carolina's Ring* and, after I told him about The Ring Trilogy and my plan to establish a brand through the books, Pat joked that he'd never had a brand. Of course, Pat did have a brand—and a band of devoted readers unlike any author. His legendary book signings still serve as a testament to his brand (and those legions of readers) who would stand in line for hours to have a book signed, when Pat made them feel like they were the only person there. I was at several of those signings, where I learned how writers should be with their readers. I hope to have those kinds of lines at some of my signings someday. You can bet I'll look each reader in the eye, just like Pat.

I do not want to repeat the admittedly long acknowledgments for *Virginia's Ring*, but practically everyone mentioned there could be included here as well (though we've sadly lost too many of them since its publication, including several brother Rats from my great VMI class, the Class of 1983). I hope everyone reading *Carolina's Ring* will read or re-read the acknowledgments in *Virginia's Ring*; it provides much insight into both books.

My writing life has changed greatly since I wrote *Virginia's Ring*, including co-authoring travel books about Charleston and Savannah and a move to beloved Beaufort, South Carolina. Most of *Carolina's Ring* was written in Beaufort (ironically, in Pat's longtime book-lined office), and the book was greatly influenced by our new lives in the Lowcountry and all of South Carolina.

Thanks first and foremost to Pat's most wonderful wife, bestselling author Cassandra King. She provided the perfect place to write and so much more. Great love.

Next, the Conroy clan continues to be supportive of my various efforts to keep Pat's legacy alive through his words, mentorship, and so much more. Thanks to Kathy Conroy Harvey and Bobby Joe Harvey, Mike and Jeannie Conroy, Tim and Terrye Conroy, Jim and Janice Conroy, Barbara Conroy, Jessica Conroy, Melissa Conroy, Megan Conroy, and Susannah Ansley Conroy. And thanks also to the extended Conroy contingent for their help with the next Seldon Ink book project, *An Appetite for Life: Travels with Conroy*.

Pat's legacy includes playing a large role in the thriving literary scene in Beaufort, including the Pat Conroy Literary Center, where Executive Director Jonathan Haupt has been a huge help to me and many other writers near and far (just like Pat). Thanks so much to the many members of our constantly growing Beaufort tribe, including the aforementioned Cassandra King and Kathy Conroy Harvey; Marly Rusoff (who lovingly represented *Carolina's Ring*) and Mihai Radulescu; John Warley (Citadel Class of 1967) and Marilyn Harcharik; Roxanne Cheney; Rob Warley and Jim Hare; Kit and

Louis Bruce; Scott (Citadel Class of 1967) and Susan Graber; Bernie and Martha Schein; Maggie Schein and Jonathan Hannah; Rebecca Bruff; Donna and Ray Armer; Mary Martha Greene; Bren McClain; Edie Smith and Gene Rugala; Don and Donna Altman; Katie and Pete Masalin (Citadel Class of 1983); Brad Fleming; Beaufort Mayor Stephen Murray; former Beaufort mayor Billy Keyserling; Peach Morrison; Jim (VMI Class of 1993) and Heather Stone; Hugh Gouldthorpe (VMI Class of 1961) and Nelle Pender; and Nancy Ritter, a fellow writer who was a very helpful advance reader and supporter of *Carolina's Ring*.

Paige Williams in Lexington, Virginia, was also an astute advance reader of *Carolina's Ring*, as well as *Virginia's Ring*. Paige and her husband, Jay (a VMI classmate), now own a wonderful independent bookstore in Lexington called Downtown Books. You can bet they've sold a lot of signed copies of *Virginia's Ring* at Downtown Books, and I can't wait to share *Carolina's Ring* with their loyal customers.

Thanks also to my VMI brother Rat Brent Dunahoe and his lovely wife, Lisa. Brent also read an early draft and many revised sections involving Marines, giving me great insight into the lives (and deaths) of Marines. Semper fi, sir. Aforementioned Citadel grad, Conroy classmate, fellow author, and Beaufort bud John Warley fulfilled a similar role with my portrayal of The Citadel, including a great tour of the fabled campus and much fact-checking and advice. That said, any mistakes with my treatment of the Marine Corps and The Citadel in *Carolina's Ring* are mine alone.

Thanks again to literary agent extraordinaire Marly Rusoff for shepherding my manuscript to Köehler Books up in Virginia. And thanks to John Koehler, Joe Coccaro, and Danielle Koehler at Köehler Books for making my words shine.

Back in Beaufort, there's Cele. Always. Thank you for marching forth with me, Carolina, and Virginia. Great life. Great love.